INGRATITUDE

D0166521

INGRATITUDE

YING CHEN

TRANSLATED

FROM

THE

FRENCH

BY

CAROL VOLK

UNIVERSITY OF CALIFORNIA PRESS
Berkeley   Los Angeles   London

University of California Press
Berkeley and Los Angeles, California

University of California Press, Ltd.
London, England

First California Paperback Printing, 1999

Translation copyright © 1998 by Carol Volk
French text copyright © 1995 by Lémeac Éditeur, Montreal
All rights reserved. Published by arrangement with
Farrar, Straus & Giroux, Inc.
Library of Congress catalog card number: 98-071376
Designed by Abby Kagan

First published in French as L'Ingratitude in 1995 by
Lémeac Éditeur, Montreal, and Actes Sud, Paris
First American edition, 1998

Library of Congress Cataloging-in-Publication Data
Chen, Ying, 1961–
    [Ingratitude. English]
    Ingratitude / Ying chen ; translated from the French by Carol Volk.
        p.   cm.
    ISBN 0-520-22013-7 (pbk. : alk. paper)
    1. Mother and child—Fiction.   2. Parent and adult child—Fiction.
    3. Death—Fiction.   I. Volk. Carol.   II. Title.
PQ3919.2.C532I643   1999
843–dc21   99-20035
                                                            CIP

Printed in the United States of America

08   07   06   05   04   03   02   01   00   99
     10   9   8   7   6   5   4   3   2   1

The paper used in this publication meets the minimum requirements
of ANSI/NISO Z39.48-1992 (R 1997) (Permanence of Paper). ♾

INGRATITUDE

THEY THROW MY BODY ONTO A ROLLING COT IN THE middle of a windowless white room. Their movements are brusque. They treat me like a criminal. When Mother's not around, they don't hide their disgust.

They tend to respect the dead more than the living. By becoming less human, and especially less fragile, from one day to the next the dead are considered more intelligent, more talented, more virtuous, and therefore worthier. But it's different in my case. My death is a disgrace beyond measure because I condemned myself to it, I carried out my own sentence. They're angry with me for not loving them enough, for fleeing their cherished domain. They will not chisel my name on a stone as they do for the others. On the contrary, they are eager to wipe me off the face of the earth. But there are plenty of other bodies to burn. On the way to the void, just like anywhere else, you have to get in line, remember that patience is a virtue, wait with a smile.

While I wait, a spider expands its territory on the ceiling and people come to see me. Along with the scent of incense heartfelt sobs and strange stammering voices rise:

"Still so young."

"And so pretty too."

"But what ideas . . . They say she left a strange letter, did you know that?"

". . . her poor mother."

It seems, then, that they went so far as to dig through the trash at the Happiness Café, and that Mother may have been lucky enough to read my letter. But isn't all this childish? The fact is, a letter won't have any more of an effect on her. The shell of her brain doesn't open to admit guilt. My death alone is enough to prove that she's innocent and I'm more of an ingrate than ever. I crossed a line forbidden to the young. Mother doesn't want to know about death, just as she didn't want to know about the men I liked. To die young is to violate the divine law. It's more immoral than showing your legs.

"Stay with us a little longer, please," Grandmother says to me. "We can't stand for you to bury your soul's torments in this endless silence. You have to speak. Criticize your poor mother if you like, criticize everyone, insult me all you want. But speak! Lay your grief on our heads. You'll have an easier journey that way, and for us it's the only consolation . . ."

Then she rests a hand on Mother's shoulder. By some miracle, Mother doesn't move, she tolerates this enemy hand.

"I would have preferred to go in her place," murmurs Grandmother, "to go before her."

Mother stops crying. She considers this for a few moments, then nods in agreement. I see her lips moving. Though I can hardly hear, I can guess her words: yes, Mother-in-law, you are rarely right, but on this point I agree with you . . . you should have gone before her.

I take a deep breath and hold it to give myself weight. I dive down. I want to get closer to Mother. I too would like to place a hand on her inaccessible shoulder. But the smoke keeps pushing me back. On the border between life and death, this smoke stands between us like a guard at his post. The smell of the incense suffocates me, its smoke blinds me. I realize what I have done. I am an exile now. It is impossible for me to return, even for an instant, with the honest intention of touching Mother's shoulder one last time. Already she is far, far away, imprisoned in this bare room, leaning over my body and trying to recognize it, a body she never recognized before.

I THINK MY SOLUTION WAS A GOOD ONE AFTER ALL. I had to betray her, with her voice like a siren and her forehead of iron. Our relationship had no spark. We were like an old couple for whom everything had become limp, predictable, rotten. We needed an abrupt separation, a vigorous uprooting to rediscover each other, even if only to abandon each other forever.

Everything happens as anticipated. She cries over my soiled body. My face is the color of dust. She now has to face up to this hard truth: she can't calculate and arrange everything to suit herself, and things don't always turn out for the best, in spite of her or thanks to her. I'm out of reach for her now. She has lost me. Everyone knows about her loss. From now on, when the conversation turns to children she'll shut her mouth. She won't put on the airs of an expert, saying: "Upbringing is very important, you know." She'll no longer have the pleasure of flaunting her experience as a mother, the rules she has established over the years and applied rigorously to correct my perverse nature. No one will even speak of children in her presence. People will pity her. From now on they will tell themselves that this mother's methods may be suspect. They won't listen to her anymore. And all this because of me. I shattered her glory, all by myself! I declared her competency, her strength, null and void. I forced her to resign from her position as a mother. I annihilated her.

I will have surprised her with what I have done. She probably still remembers how fearful and withdrawn I was in her presence. She'll question the notion that I lacked intelligence and character, since she herself would never dare do such a thing. Ordinary people don't do away with themselves. They cling to life, to any life. Even if they sometimes grow tired of others and especially of themselves, they don't admit it. They hide behind rigid smiles. Their bursts of laughter ring false. They stay alive. They don't dare utter so much as a mournful word. They avoid doing anything outrageous. They're afraid of the consequences, of being considered abnormal and becoming very ugly as they die. They remain hopeful, even if they can clearly see that today is never better than yesterday and that there is nothing good to expect from tomorrow. Mother will tell herself she was dealing with a unique individual. She'll blame herself for not understanding me, despite all these years of housing, feeding, washing, scolding, and dressing me, of turning me this way and that. I am a child—for I will forever be her child—who is not like the others. A girl who seemed ordinary on the surface but who deep down was brave, who was way ahead of her. She'll have the impression of having missed the last bus in the twilight of her life. Reading my recovered letter, she'll understand—too late—that this bus waited for her, silently, all these regrettable years, in the hope of taking her to a garden of promise. Now that bus has left without her, fulfilling its destiny in what may have been a voluntary accident. Next she will repent of her whims and her tyranny. Her insides will clench as she contemplates the empty path before her. Since she doesn't have the courage to die, she will continue to drag her feet, alone, exhausted and without hope.

I SHOULD HAVE ACTED SOONER ON THIS PLAN, WHICH I'd nourished for so long, nourished from the moment I knew I was condemned to have a mother and a father. Life would have been easier without them. When I went to school, I envied the orphans, free to play as much as they wanted and repeat as many grades as they could. I wrote broadsides against the father of our feudalism. Down with Kong-Zi, I wrote, or our civilization will sink in the mud of its origins, our generation will be lost at the hands of our parents, and I shall die at my mother's feet! The teacher was proud of me.

I wasn't afraid of throwing myself out the window or of having my head crushed by a bus. "To be or not to be" didn't seem like an intelligent question to me. I didn't find many intelligent things in books. Otherwise, I would have had more respect for Father, who wrote books. For once, Mother agreed with me. She thought I was wasting my time reading their yellowed pages: Kong-Zi may have been wrong about everything else, but when he said that ignorance was a virtue for women, he wasn't far from the truth. I would smile when she said this. A smile she said could harden the tenderest of hearts. A smile that seemed to say: Yes, I know, Mother, only ignorance can deepen our sleep and inner peace and thus enhance our feminine charms.

And that wasn't the only thing I mocked. I didn't want to go anywhere near psychologists, who considered everyone sick. I thought they were sick themselves, sicker than Father, a professor twenty-four hours a day. Those people had a very particular view of things. They looked at a person and saw only the brain. And the brain is a lump of moist flesh, a lump of flesh no more beautiful than other lumps of flesh, nor any cleaner. I was a little afraid of falling into their hands, of having my brain functions checked out if the suicide attempt failed. If it succeeded, my greatest fear concerned my friends. Their pity and confusion would be hard for my soul to bear. But did my soul deserve greater consideration than my body? When Chairman Mao said that Dr. Bethune had sacrificed his life for the Chinese people and that his death was therefore heavier to bear than mountains, he was talking about his soul, of course. Yet Grandmother claimed that souls were all lighter than bodies.

Now, floating over this dizzying smoke of incense, I see that Grandmother was right, even if people don't want to believe it. They cling to life the way feathers cling to a bird, without realizing how little they weigh. They hate those who'd rather set sail, abandon a life they don't own, jump into the void, which at least has the advantage of being endless. They accuse them of cowardice to prove their own bravery. They take the liberty of judging the dead. As a result, the dead are seen differently from one era to the next: heavy or light, heroic or cowardly, valuable or useless, virtuous or immoral. Death has become just like anything else, something to which they assign a price that varies with their mood.

I WAS BURNING WITH THE DESIRE TO SEE MOTHER suffer at the sight of my corpse. Suffer to the point of vomiting up her own blood. An inconsolable pain. Life would be slipping through her fingers and her descendants would be escaping her. As my body began to rot in the warmth of the days, her genes would stop circulating in my veins, would get lost at the bottom of the uniform earth. She would no longer have a child. Her only daughter would be flying far away from her, as a mortal gust of wind rips past a tree, shaking it mercilessly.

For best results I needed patience. It would be important to leave her a very gentle letter, saying that I truly loved her, that she was my only true love, and that I was going to die for her. This wasn't easy. Mother was so perceptive. I had to try my damnedest to win her trust. My love for her was what she wanted most in life, and at the same time, the last thing in the world she believed in. So I had to be careful. It would take imagination. I had to dream up a fictional mother, adopt a reasonable tone, apply a touch of restrained tenderness here and there. I would choose my words and phrases carefully. They should be neither too sweet nor too bitter. A few tears would be useful to bring out the scent of the paper. But they had to be chilled before serving . . .

THE HAPPINESS CAFÉ SEEMED VERY WELCOMING.

There were grains of rice stuck to the tables and chicken bones scattered beneath the chairs. I sat near the window. The proprietress bounded toward me, her face opened up like a cabbage.

"I came here," I confessed, "because I didn't know where to go."

"That's just fine," she said. "It's fine not to know where to go. You always get somewhere anyway. To a good place, I mean."

She looked at me attentively for a moment or two. She wanted to know if my parents were in good health, if I had someone in my life, and so on.

"I have an important letter to write."

Annoyed and apologetic, she headed for the other tables. "Don't worry, I'm not going to bother you. I mean, I don't bother intellectuals."

I took out a sheet of paper. I diligently traced the word *Mother* on it. But I immediately had to put down the pen. The word had gotten soaked in a reddish twilight that made me nauseous. I looked out the window. The pedestrians parading past were blocking my view. They came to this festive street, smartly dressed, to give themselves the illusion of living a cosmopolitan life. Taxis passed frequently, proudly overtaking the bicyclists and unable to restrain themselves from honking in triumph. These crisp, high-pitched sounds reminded me of Mother's voice.

MOTHER, WHO had an excellent memory, had forgotten my birthday again. The pain I had caused her in coming into the world didn't help her to remember the date. Her belly bore a dark line in the shape of a snake. Sometimes, in the public baths, we eyed each other in silence. I asked no questions and she pretended not to notice my embarrassment. I came out of there! Out of that soft, dirty belly, swollen with fat. Better to be born from a stone or an anonymous plant. But the dark line on this stranger's belly cried out to me: You can't get away from me, I'm the one who formed you, your body and your spirit, with my flesh and my blood—you're mine, all mine! According to Grandmother, I was late in coming. I had fought as best I could against Mother's bowels, which were pushing me imperiously down a slippery slope that would lead me to the brink of the void, to this borrowed life, to my fate as the child of this woman. Yes, Mother's arms awaited me as her body hastened to expel me. She cursed my stubbornness for ten hours or more before they opened her up.

STILL, MOTHER always said it was a thousand times harder to watch me grow than to give birth to me. Because as I grew I resembled her less and less. Nor did I resemble my father, for that matter. Everyone said I had my father's forehead and my mother's cheeks. But so long as my face had not taken form, we couldn't be sure. Temperamentally I was almost their opposite. For example, I could never utter Mother's favorite saying without blushing down to my throat: "I'm doing this for your own good." Wasn't wanting to look out for the welfare of others an attempt at rape and pillage? Nor could I reason like my father with *for*s and *therefore*s, *consequently*s and *notwithstanding*s without going mad. All this was hard for Mother to take. While I stared at her belly through the splash of the shower, she examined my body with the demanding and lucid eyes of a stranger. I sometimes had the impression that she wanted to swallow me whole, remake me in her body and give birth to me all over again, with a physique, a personality, and a mind more to her liking.

I sought in vain to please her. I tried to be good. I did the housework, ate lightly, and devoted eight hours a week to learning to sew. I rarely went out. I closed my eyes to men and my ears to their affairs. I gently joined the chattering of my aunts and the neighborhood women. I said okay to everything with an unfailing smile. I was practically faultless. A perfect daughter. A daughter worthy of her mother. But you can't really please a mother after you hurt her by coming into the world. You can't repair that oh so violent wound to the body which later becomes a wound to the heart. Mother repaid all my efforts by calling me a little hypocrite. She believed, and rightly so, that deep down I was exasperated by women's work, that I loved to eat, was sensitive to men and critical by nature. She considered me pitiful, disappointed as she was by all these lowly traits. Sometimes, after scolding me during a meal, before leaving the table, all of a sudden she would mumble: "It's not worth it." And I would ask her: "What's not worth it, Mother?" She wouldn't reply. I imagined she regretted having wanted a child. She especially regretted that I, and not another, had emerged from her body. But in the name of the family's honor, she felt obliged to keep an eye on me anyway, to avoid scandal as much as possible and ensure me a good future, which is to say a proper marriage, perhaps like hers to my father.

I, HOWEVER, DID NOT FORGET MY BIRTHDAY. GIVEN the choice, I would have preferred to die in the private warmth of the maternal body. To die before any consciousness developed. To transform myself into streams of blood that would survive in the black earth. Mother may have shared that wish when things were going badly between us. At the very thought that, on the day I was born, Mother, still lying in her bloody bed, had clasped me in her arms with a creator's pride, a giver's grace, and an owner's caution, I couldn't help but believe that the day of my birth was already the day of my defeat. No one had asked my opinion before casting me out into the world. So I hoped they would at least allow me to choose the time of my departure.

That's why I never celebrated my birthday—it was my way of forgetting as best I could the subtle humiliation that had been forced upon me, of not reopening the wound I carried in my head from the beginning, just as Mother carried the scar on her belly. Sometimes, at my worst, I would cry to myself: "I don't owe you anything, Mother! You've always wanted me to be just like you, you live in my body without any invitation, and you decide so much of my fate! You're such a tyrant!" My doctor kept asking me about the state of my parents' health, as if my own life depended on them! I was finally beginning to understand that my life didn't fully belong to me, and I hated my parents for it, especially Mother. Why give a life knowing almost from the start how it was going to end? I couldn't stand it. I had lived as my mother's child. I had to die differently. I would end my days my way. When I was no longer anything, I would be me.

Mother suspected my dark thoughts. She wore herself out correcting this ingratitude by punishing me, by preventing me from sleeping at night and by forcing me to write little critiques of myself. She believed, nonetheless, that while mountains could move, human beings never changed. She knew how to judge people as young as three years old. According to Mother, I had been passive as a child, which is to say I had been obedient and fearful of her, a state that made her both happy and unhappy. She was suspicious of my love for her. Without my knowing why, her presence in the house stifled me as much as a stormy sky or a sad song. Often, I stopped playing when she appeared, frozen in place, wishing I could run away. I told my cousins that Mother was strict, but they didn't agree. That meant I had preconceptions about Mother. According to her, a child who loves his parents would never have an opinion about them. Yet I could never manage to love my parents without judgment and without qualifications. Since they were no better-looking and no smarter than other people's parents, I didn't flatter them. I didn't want to lie. I simply hoped to hide behind my obedience.

I was ungrateful toward them because I was ungrateful for the life they had given me. Maybe I could love them a little if I thought of them simply as friends I'd encountered along life's way who had had nothing to do with my birth and survival. Alas, they'd throw themselves in the river if they heard such insolence. Wasn't the simple fact of being born and staying alive already great cause for joy? What more could you want? I always gave you the essentials, Mother said.

•　　•　　•

BUT I mustn't write to her with this disarming frankness which, upon my death, would be the best consolation to her. What could she do when the sky itself decided to punish this wicked girl who rebelled against the order of things? The loss of a daughter like me wouldn't shake her status as a mother. She would remain my mother. She would continue to enjoy the advantages of a mother: scolding me, pitying me, teaching me lessons that begin: "You should have . . ." She would continue to do all this as much as she wanted, without having to put up with my sulking anymore. But I wouldn't give her the satisfaction. I had to calm down. The trick was to inspire not her hatred but her sorrow. Hatred passes, whereas sorrow remains . . .

THE PROPRIETRESS OF THE HAPPINESS CAFÉ HAD THE nerve to call me an intellectual. Under other circumstances, I would have been furious. But that day I didn't make a fuss. Even though I was still alive, my reflexes were already dulled, my nerves were so relaxed that I felt neither angry nor sad. Besides, it was true that I probably looked like my father, sitting at the table with my paper and pen.

FATHER SPENT almost all his time at his desk. He dove into books just as he had in the past. Except that, while his body was constantly moving, the pages rarely turned. A gust of wind came in the window and sent his papers flying. His glasses slipped down his nose. He had to arrange the papers, readjust his glasses with his left hand, and hold a pen in his right, a pen which, for hours at a time, left no mark on the paper. He had to struggle against so many things. Against his glasses, his pen, and his papers. Against the wind and fatigue. Against the illogical images, perhaps, that paraded through his head. Against my exaggeratedly muffled steps and Mother's shouting. With his air of seriousness, his back straight, his neck bent forward, and his right hand on his forehead, he was the scholar incarnate.

Ever since the day he was hit by a truck and came home with the consent of his doctors, who believed he had survived the accident miraculously intact, Father no longer wrote his polemical essays. His readers still remembered the elegance of his style, some nostalgically, others with malice. They recalled the conviction of his arguments, and most of all that manner all his own of explaining everything with "isms." In the beginning, Father still went regularly to the university. But since he seemed to be forgetting his material, the administration offered him an early retirement.

Mother was happy about this turn of events. It's too dangerous to mess with politics in this country, she declared, we don't live in America, you have to take your own particular circumstances into account. For some time now, since they had started talking about opening up to foreigners, Mother had tried to fit the new situation to her old beliefs: happily, her country and her people were different from others; nonetheless, in order to stand up to the new influences and to remain ourselves more than ever, it was necessary to fortify our minds and strengthen our immune system. "Your father was such an alert man," she would add. "Who knows whether this accident wasn't an attempted murder! You have to keep your eye on these kids, they're crazy today, they think they can look down on everyone, their teachers, their parents, their ancestors. But believe me, the day they kill their past, they'll cry for their future!"

As a result, every night on her way to the bathroom, Mother took a slight detour to check that the door to the apartment was bolted. Under the pressure of her fingers, the lock let out a scream that made the whole family jump.

Mother didn't confess all her thoughts. She despised Father's work for other reasons. On Sunday mornings, she raised her voice as she ordered me to accompany her to the market: "You come with me, your father's too busy!" She didn't dare say anything more out of deference toward intellectual work. Nonetheless, she would wait on the threshold a few moments. Only after noting that the tomblike silence persisted in Father's study would she slam the door behind her. Perhaps Mother saw his retirement as a chance to reconquer her man and defeat all his books and papers.

I WENT TO SEE FATHER IN HIS STUDY. I BROUGHT HIM
a cup of tea. He was in the habit of drinking tea toward
the end of the day. In my heart I had a feeling as soft
as the setting sun, a filial piety that I wanted to express
to him for the last time. Yet I had lived in fear of both-
ering him, of distracting him with my trifles, of tearing
him away from thoughts that were liable to affect the
forward or backward march of the planet. His work was
indispensable to the welfare of the human race, or at
least to the fame of our family. So I walked on tiptoe,
without a sound, ashamed of my existence and trying to
make myself as small as possible. I felt guilty for having
to interrupt the evolution of the world even just a bit,

in my own home, with a ridiculous cup of tea. But at the moment I planned to gently set the cup on the desk, my hands rebelled: they shook so strongly that drops of boiling water leapt to my wrist. I dropped the cup on a sheet of paper, and a damp circle formed on it. I blushed. But I didn't say I was sorry.

As usual, he turned to me, surprised. He looked at me as if he didn't know me. Then he turned away. He still had his pen in his hand. I knew he wouldn't touch his tea until he was alone again. But I didn't want to leave. I had a lot to say to him. I hesitated, not knowing where to begin. I thought it was a little bit because of him that Mother and I got along like fire and water. Had he been less of a university professor, had he been as concerned about what was on our dinner table as about what was happening in Vietnam or Yugoslavia, had he gone to the market more often than to the museum, had he deigned to be a little more attentive to Mother and what she was doing in the house—indeed, how many times a week did she clean the floor? wasn't the dust that accumulated in our home as important as the ruins of a distant civilization?—Mother wouldn't have been so dependent on my presence and on my virtue. If only Father could have shared with me some of the enormous responsibility for making this woman happy, this woman who had done so much for him and for me, I could have breathed easier and perhaps lived longer. Alas, Father was made of oil and, like oil, kept separate from water, pushing fire to madness. In some sense, it was he who had made an enemy for me. It wasn't fair to take revenge only on Mother. But what else could I do? Father was an intellectual, and thus imperturbable. My suicide interested him less than the assassination of an American president. You can only hit those in the range of fire.

Everything was in order then. Everything was the same today as it was yesterday. Father would never come to the market with Mother and me on Sunday morning. He would never say a word to me when I'd bring him his tea and the vacant look in his eyes as he gazed at me would never be filled. Since the accident, in fact, this vacancy seemed to expand more and more like an open sore that covers the entire body. In the past, his vehemence in debate and his success in his field had been my great consolation. Since I understood nothing about what he did, I had admired him for his facility with language and his abstract mind. If, at home, he wasn't a model husband or a tender father, at least he had been a good player with words in the outside world. Everything in his office, the books, papers, pens, all these things that boggled my mind, were just toys for him. He could speak of a book with his eyes closed. But upon addressing his colleagues, he knew how to open them just enough to allow a glimmer of intelligence to peer through, to show his sparkling teeth while heightening his tone, to knowingly roll his tongue in order to bring out his standard accent, to modulate his voice to moving effect, to agitate his hands with restraint, to wait a second or two over a fine expression . . . Seeing him speak, I used to think of a well-made doll, both lucid and devoted. He had been the game itself. I preferred Father the speaker to Father the reader or thinker.

Alas, he no longer wrote and rarely spoke. I still found critiques of his old articles from time to time. Sometimes they loved him and sometimes they hated him. Since the accident, his students and readers had stopped coming to visit. But Father still spent his days in his study, still drank his afternoon tea, the paleness of his papers reflected in his hair.

I LEFT him without a word, without a farewell. Without touching his hand, that oh so indifferent hand, already foreign to me.

BUT HOW COULD I HOLD ANYTHING AGAINST HIM?
After the accident, Father was capable neither of work
nor of affection. He was half dead. Or at least he had
become . . . weak. His weakness softened Mother. A good
person should have pity, she would say.

This moral Mother had taught me nearly doused the
flame of my judgment. At which point I developed a
horror of the weak, of people like my father whose weakness had become a weapon, a green light for every cruelty, an excuse for their cowardice. I kept away from
them as from sleeping snakes, against which any act of
self-defense would be immoral.

IT WAS clear that Mother no longer had any pity for me—perhaps the only sentiment she had ever been capable of. The only valid sentiment. The proof of a good heart. I knew the taste of her heart. She had spoken several times of driving a knife into her chest, of removing her bleeding heart and showing me how sick it was over me. Can't you see, she would say, that my heart is pickled in salt?

The salt was my silence, a source of suffering for Mother. Sometimes she would force me to sit next to her and talk. Yet she wouldn't say anything. She wouldn't look at me. She would sit up straight in her chair. Mother's back must never bend. She would knit while awaiting my words. She always had something to knit. We would listen to the clicking of the needles, our nerves tensed. The more time passed, the more desperate I became. I rummaged through my mind in vain. I didn't dare tell her funny stories (they might be immoral), or sad ones (they might make her even more serious). Mother had decided never to laugh in front of me. Any carefree gesture on her part risked compromising her power. Authority is the guarantee of a good education, she would say.

Once I caught her chatting and laughing with a woman from the neighborhood. It was a sunny afternoon.

She was on her bedroom balcony. Her entire body was radiant; an orange light crowned her head. I couldn't believe my eyes. The mother I had so often dreamed of was here, at long last, that dazzling and divine woman. I imagined myself in her arms, my forehead nestled between her breasts, my nose filled with the rich odor of her skin—Mother smelled like the local river. She noticed me standing there and walked toward me. She emerged from the light but now she had clouded over. I stood on the threshold, still confused and happy. "Mother . . . " I stammered. I must have looked stupid, because she immediately hid her smile, erasing any sign of life from her face, and began to ask me about my homework. I was very jealous of the neighbor.

Thus, her heart was being preserved in my salty silence. A good heart was essential to her mission of educating me. She was determined in her task, because it was her domain, her way of participating in creation and making her mark on the world.

Now I missed Mother's pity. In the past, I liked getting sick more than anything. When I was sick she would lean over my bed to talk to me. This worried me; I was afraid her back would break. She would place a cool hand on my forehead to take my temperature and a trace of a smile would affix itself to her lips. The same smile, probably, as on the day I was born. A serious, committed, and satisfied smile. I would hold back my tears, scarcely breathing, for fear that my breath would chase away her smile. How I regretted my robust health.

But for some time now Mother had no longer classified me among the weak, because I had grown up and become . . . a young person. Mother didn't like young people. By "They're young," she meant: "They're stupid" or "They're dangerous." She had much to forgive youth, and she didn't do it easily. This didn't stop her from regretting her own youth. "Ah," she would sigh, "if I could just start over!" That's why she didn't accept that others should live too much: they want to change everything, youth isn't enough for them, they want everything, everything! They want more than we had, more than their parents, who had so little, who want so little . . .

This made me feel ashamed of my youth. To please Mother, I had to grow old. I wanted to be her age, the enviable age of fifty. At fifty, according to Kong-Zi, one becomes perfect. One stands straight, one is no longer confused, and one understands one's destiny. And the more I thought about it, the older I became. The question of death haunted me. I saw it as the only possibility of deliverance, of avoiding fate before encountering it, before the age of fifty. Sometimes I would stroll in a park at night and try to reflect on life from the perspective of an old lady. Life was like moonlight on a pond. It scared me. I realized that you should never reflect on life or you won't be able to do anything, whether it's eating a chicken leg, going out with men, or putting up with your mother. On the contrary, to survive you had to be content with your youth, be daring enough to plunge into the pond where the moon waited, where light reigned. Alas, I was incapable of such a thing. I stayed at the water's edge, in the darkness. Time rushed toward me, wisdom ate at my nerves, the shadow of Mother covered my body. I didn't move. During what she called my ascetic lapses, I couldn't hear Mother giving me orders. I must have had a blank look that irritated her. "You're like your father!" she would say, clenching her teeth.

This phrase burst over my skull like thunder. I resembled my father! I'd have a bald head and dry skin like him when I was his age. And a mind as insensitive as his. Already the Sunday morning market bored me stiff. Mother bored me too. Life was passing me by. It went on its merry way, indifferent to my presence, taking with it those who joined in and abandoning those who stood on the side of the road. I saw myself alone with my father, trailing behind in life, surrounded by dusty papers. I saw myself dead in the midst of life.

SO GRANDMOTHER AND MOTHER, TWO WOMEN WHO have despised each other for so many years on my account, will cry together over my tomb. I want Mother to shed her tears, many tears, just as she shed her blood the day I was born. That's the price a mother must pay. As for Grandmother, she paid dearly for her own child. Tears, she says, are a source of life. She has cried too many for my father. She doesn't have many left.

Yet at the sight of my body, tears come despite her and flow with frightening abandon. Grandmother lowers her head, as if to expose her thinning hair and its transparent whiteness. In the past, long, long ago, I used to watch her comb her hair. Every morning she'd dip her comb in an oily solution. Then she would comb and comb her locks, which fell abundantly to her waist, until they were as shiny as black silk. Finally, slowly, she would roll this delicate mass into a great ball, which she affixed to the back of her head. She always combed her hair standing up, in front of the redwood table near the window. Her mirror, rusted by time, would catch the sun. "I can't see myself clearly," she would murmur. But she would smile, happy, about what I didn't know. At these moments, I understood why everyone said that Grandmother was a beautiful woman, and why Mother despised her.

"When your hair is too long," Mother would say, "your intelligence is short."

"But Father's hair is shorter than yours," I would note. "Is he smarter?"

"Well, he's an exception," she'd respond crisply.

Finally, one day, Grandmother had her hair cut. To become smarter, it seems. But for other reasons too. As her hair changed color and looked like the dawn more than the noonday sun, she had to sit down to comb it. And she needed me to bring her this or that. Later, she started asking me to tend to it. Her hair was still very soft, it flowed in my hands, slippery as water. Grandmother was never satisfied with what I did. "Gently," she would complain, "don't forget that hair has a spirit!" But the day came when the spirit vanished. It was a beautiful spring morning. The sun had the same languid softness as twenty years earlier. Grandmother finally noticed that her face resembled her old mirror. And she abandoned the daily ritual she had bestowed on her hair for so many years.

From then on she advised me to wear my hair long. "The biggest mistake your father ever made," she began when Mother wasn't around, "was to marry a woman with unpresentable hair. They say the quality of the hair is a reflection of the quality of the person . . . Fortunately you look more like your father." Grandmother spoke these words with the tone of those who believe they belong to a better race and feel their superiority trampled by the rabble—a tone that would prompt Mother to lose control and cry with rage.

As for me, regarding the quality of hair, I have nothing to say to Grandmother; I will have nothing to tell her even when her spirit joins me one of these days. Because I will always remember her hair, which used to flow through my fingers, like a liquid that's still warm but already destined for the earth.

SUMMER CONTINUES TO CORRUPT AUTUMN WITH A
strange heat. People are still wearing short-sleeved shirts.
Fans are flapping nervously. A smell of urine emanates
from my body. They finally promise to burn me as soon
as possible. But now Mother and Grandmother are en-
gaged in a pitched battle over what clothes I should be
wearing when I'm cast into the fire. Grandmother insists
that I should be dressed in a traditional winter coat, so
that I won't be cold when I arrive and the ancestors'
spirits will be hospitable. Mother thinks this is ridiculous,
an idea that could only dishonor her as the mother of
the deceased. She insists that, even dead, I should be
made presentable, as befits a proper family. Thus, my

nearly decomposed body will be sent into the fire without makeup, in a modest dress. The simmering hatred between these two women erupts, its bursts of fury fling me against the walls, into the spiderwebs.

"When she was alive," Grandmother attacks, "the little one never had decent clothing. Now that she's leaving us, try to let her go in grace."

"How can she leave us peacefully," sneers Mother, "when she comes from a family that has a rule for everything?"

Grandmother doesn't seem to want to back down this time.

"That's right, we know the rules that killed my granddaughter."

"Watch it—she's *my* daughter and this is *my* business."

Mother's features harden. I see, to my great disappointment, that my death is not helping to change her. She argues with even more gusto. Her own life goes on without me. She's not the type to be crushed by the whims of fate. Instead of dragging her down, misfortune stimulates and fortifies her. At night, she doesn't sleep. She dreams. The suicide hypothesis seems unfounded to her, and particularly damaging to her reputation and mine. She has the extraordinary ability to keep only ideas that are flattering to her in her head and to expel the slightest unpleasant doubt. She knows how to ignore what she wants to ignore. And she is convinced that the truth can only be what is best for her. She has the character of the invincible.

And in the calm of night, her thoughts drift in another direction. She seeks a link between my death and my father's accident. She wonders if it wasn't the same vehicle that struck us both. She even tries to explain the motives for these accidents. She thinks to the sound of my father's snoring. Every one of her nerves is awake. She is suffering no longer. She is forgetting me. Hardly has my body begun to stink than I am forgotten.

IF I HADN'T HAD THE WHEREWITHAL TO PERSIST, MY plan would have remained just that, a plan. So many things got in my way. For one, Chun came to dinner for the first time. I had been unable to dissuade Mother from inviting him or to keep him from accepting the invitation. Mother was choosing her future son-in-law, and he wanted to make the acquaintance of his future mother-in-law. Their meeting was out of my hands.

To be polite, Mother bought pork. She and I spent that afternoon in the kitchen. I washed the meat and she cut it into chunks and dipped them in soy sauce. I was so focused on the pleasure of eating the meat that I almost forgot about the guest.

Mother would have been pleased to know that I was thinking more about the meat than the man. According to her, a passionate love was dangerous. It could alter my memory, make me forget my origins, abandon my mother and devote myself to a young stranger who had done nothing for me. It naturally implied ingratitude.

WHEN SHE spoke of passionate love, Mother was no doubt alluding to Hong-Qi, whom she and I so despised. Because of him, I was so despondent that it would have taken me several years or more to get back on my feet, maybe the rest of my life had it lasted long enough.

Hong-Qi was my first love. We met at the university. It was spring. We were drunk on the damp, scented air. I was eighteen; he was twenty-one. All this was enough for a first love. At the sound of his voice my heart leapt to my throat. He told me things I didn't dare say to myself for fear of being banal. At that age, you're afraid of being banal. Hong-Qi judged girls by their virtue and boys by their family. He was proud of his father, who had seen clearly through the whirlwinds of history— which is to say he had given his life to the Liberation Army—and who had become a top administrator after the Victory and before his retirement. To me, he was a true hero. Hong-Qi himself had a voice like beautiful music; he was tall with narrow shoulders, bowlegs, and thick glasses. I found him handsome, even though my girlfriends didn't seem to agree. I felt truly happy with him.

It was a big event for me and, soon, for Mother. I wanted to comply with Mother's wishes in everything, but I still didn't know her views on love. We had never spoken about love between a man and a woman; I didn't dare ask her questions and sought in vain to learn whatever I could. Until I was eighteen I knew nothing of what happened between a couple. I wasn't really conscious of being a woman. I wore ludicrous clothing that Mother made for me—innocence and economy were the two virtues she venerated most. About men I knew nothing until I met Hong-Qi. I thought that Mother got along well with Father, who spoke to her rarely but never contradicted her regarding family matters, family not being his domain. But since they seemed to want to stay together to their final days, I thought there must be a solid love between them, which led me to believe that, for Mother, love was a good thing. So I confided in her about my own.

This was a terrible mistake. Mother shrieked in despair. On the surface, she was upset because Hong-Qi was new to our city, a ridiculous foreigner despite his father's glorious past, a hick whose feet still smelled of the earth. But the true reason for her fury lay elsewhere.

Deep down, as she later admitted, Mother was first

and foremost shocked by the nature of my love and my obstinacy in the matter. In this world, she would say, there was no lack of men worth marrying. She even suggested that I go out with another boy of better station. By this I guessed that, since her marriage had been arranged by her parents, she had never been in a position to love a man the way I did, and that she clung to the idea that such a state of affairs was natural. Moreover, she felt she'd been deceived. Knowing that I didn't love her enough, she had thought I had an innate hardness of heart, probably inherited from my father. This illusion had sustained her all these years, the inability to love being less hurtful than the desire not to love.

She threatened to throw me out of the house if I kept seeing him. This would have caused me serious trouble when it came to public opinion, which respected parental authority and upheld family values. But I didn't have to leave home after all. Wounded by the attitude of his intended mother-in-law and refusing to bear the stigma of having kidnapped a girl from her parents, Hong-Qi brought our story to a close, without much hesitation.

MOTHER SEEMED nervous that afternoon. Was she thinking of this misadventure when I was eighteen? Or was she preparing for a new battle against the eternal future son-in-law?

CHUN SPENT A MONTH'S SALARY TO BRING GINSENG AS a gift to my parents. The advertisements linked ginseng with longevity. I told him he should just bring a little meat. It was much less expensive, and the need for meat was becoming more pressing in our family; with its price rising rapidly, my parents were trying to replace it completely with vegetables. Vegetarianism was very fashionable in the West, according to my father.

I could understand those Westerners. Having ingested since birth who knows how many tons of meat and milk products, they were now seeking prestige by eating only vegetables—this while claiming to be noble defenders of nature, animals, and many other things. But I was angry at Father for praising this experiment to Grandmother and me, descendants of a lean people who had greeted one another for centuries by asking: "Have you eaten?"

In any case, I knew my parents loved meat. That's why I thought that meat was more important to them than ginseng and that they'd rather live a happy life than a long one. But Chun laughed at my ignorance. Nothing pleased parents more than ginseng. Longevity was the most loyal wish one could make for them in this city, where young people with no place to live awaited the death of their parents so they could inherit their homes. I had to admit that my idea was too down-to-earth and that Chun knew better than I did.

Besides, I noticed that all evening he added a "don't you think?" to everything he said, even if he wasn't expecting a response.

"These dishes are marvelous," he said, addressing the entire table, "don't you think?"

Mother shrugged slightly, haughtily satisfied with his deference—the humility a man had to display to a mother-in-law in order to ask the hand of her daughter.

"Eat a little more if you like," she offered.

He took a few modest bites and murmured, "I'm really eating a lot, don't you think?"

I had warned him that Mother didn't like quiet people

or people with too many opinions. Chun had come that evening to face his first test. He considered it an important one for him, and thus for me.

He and Mother chatted. Grandmother excused herself early. Father settled into his armchair. His lips drooped, his eyelids were heavy, his dark gaze resembled the light of a broken lamp. I wiped the table, but Mother told me to leave the dishes in the sink. She made tea and served it to me with a big smile. She obviously wanted to make the young man believe that I was the family treasure and that she wouldn't let me go. He listened to her attentively, adopting a neutral, if not a slightly cool, tone when speaking of his own parents. He mentioned them only in reply to Mother's questions. Because the first thing Mother wanted to know was what type of blood flowed in the veins of this stranger who dared knock on our door. If this blood wasn't better than ours, as Mother wished it to be, at least it should be clean, virus-free, and moderate in temperament. Next, the candidate had to prove his ability to detach himself from his nest and devote himself to his new family. It's true that children should remain faithful to their parents, but Mother's son-in-law would not be like everyone else. Mother's son-in-law had other missions to accomplish, other responsibilities to assume, other masters to follow. He had to understand that his in-laws would be more important than his own parents.

Chun seemed to know the role he was playing to a T. Mother asked the questions she had prepared in advance; he responded to them, his neck stretched forward, his gaze alert, as if he were a contestant on a game show. But it was more than a game—it was a trial, practically, the stakes were so high. The future of his love depended on this evening and he knew it. But they had no further need of me. Father was beginning to snore. I ended up shutting my eyes as well. When Mother woke me, Chun was preparing to leave. Their parting words revealed nothing to me about the outcome of this encounter. Not that I was expecting results from anything anymore. I was just curious and intrigued by Mother's manners. She showed her guest out. The latter smiled again before taking his leave. Instead of an inviting "Come again," Mother simply said, "Thank you for coming."

The other responded, "Thank you for having me."

The door clicked politely shut.

HOW LUCKY to be a stranger to this house! How lucky to be Mother's would-be son-in-law and not her true son-in-law, or worse still, her son! At least Mother had been gracious to Chun. She could be gracious to everyone except the members of her own family. With them she thought politeness would be hypocritical and beside the point; her severity and slight cruelty were necessary, in fact, and constituted solid proof of her love. It was a sovereign, condescending, providential love, of course, the love of the mistress of a house who had given life and now gave orders, the love of a spider presiding over its web through its bodily substances, through a mixture of blood, spit, sweat, and tears.

WHEN HE'D GONE MOTHER AND I WASHED THE DISHES. The bowls knocked together in the water. Neither of us spoke of Chun. Mother was holding off on stating her opinion. She was avoiding taking easy swipes. She was being patient. She had time. She was thinking it over first, collecting her energy, waiting for the right moment to announce her decision, the moment when the snake would emerge from its hole of its own accord—the better to slay it cleanly, surely, and, above all, logically. This was the kind of know-how I admired in Mother. In our house, Mother's opinions were final. But I was in no hurry to know what she thought. All this was meaningless to me. Maybe it still made sense to Chun and to

Mother, but it had nothing to do with me. Marriage was no longer my only hope of escape, as I had believed in the past. No, the only other way out was . . . I stared into the sink. All I could see was the scum.

If she could have guessed what was in my head, Mother probably would have scolded me: You're always seeing the bad side of things! That was because I had suffered too many blows to embrace life with open arms. Tonight, watching Chun speak to Mother in the dim light, I'd thought I could see Hong-Qi again. How wise of him to spare himself all this pain by dumping the two of us, Mother and me—because you couldn't be with me without being with Mother, and you couldn't please Mother if you pleased me. How lucky for him to have kicked us back into our own mud, on the side of the road, a road he'd walk with his arms free from now on, his legs light and his spirit easy. No, it's not that I was a pessimist. I had simply learned to withdraw into myself and to keep my cursed tongue locked up behind my teeth. I knew what should and should not be said.

Mother had still given no commentary on Chun. Generally, she had a hard time holding back her desire to criticize every man I met or mentioned to her. This time, the delay was probably due to the ginseng, or to the suitability of the guest, or to the disturbing fact that I had long since passed the conventional age for marriage, there weren't that many eligible boys left, and I was already at risk of being devalued and ruined. I had to hurry. Marry quick, quick, people would tell me, lower your sights if you have to. But this great caution on Mother's part could also be due to the fact that I had said nothing in praise of Chun; on the contrary, I had remarked on only his flaws—minor flaws, of course. Mother loved that: lucidity and a little coldness in love. Two people together in a single bed don't tell each other their dreams. She had taught me that proverb as soon as I grew interested in romance. Mother knew other proverbs for other circumstances. For example, every time she thought I was hiding something from her, she made sure I heard this: You can't hide fire behind paper.

By making sure not to say anything good about men, by taking care to criticize them in front of Mother, I felt that the force of my love was diminishing. I had faced too early the fragility of love, and thus of life. I had realized one thing: you had to harden yourself in order to live and . . . die. A wound inflicted in youth never fully healed; you simply tried to avoid stumbling in the same place a second time. The instinct to protect yourself was stronger than the instinct to give yourself. When I was with Chun all I could think about was Mother. The sweet things he said touched me sometimes, but right away I became aware of my situation. Sublimation was impossible. I was growing old fast. Mother appreciated this type of aging, which she called maturity.

As a result, I didn't love Chun the way I had loved Hong-Qi. And yet I found him more affectionate, more handsome and intelligent. He had the virtues and flaws of an ordinary husband. With my imagination weakening, I was no longer able to exaggerate a person's strong points or ignore his weak ones, as I once had. It seemed to me that by feigning indifference to Chun to please Mother, I was telling part of the truth, though I reserved another part for him. I had developed the habit of never telling the whole truth—the habit, that is, of lying. It's easy to fashion lies from parts of the truth, or to extract truth from lies. Indeed, isn't that the game lawyers, journalists, politicians, and professors like Father play: hiding lies in one's choice of truths? When I thought carefully about the phrase "You can't hide fire behind paper," which meant that the truth cannot be hidden by a lie, I wondered if the reverse wasn't understood: a lie cannot be hidden by the truth. The power of the lie and the fragility of the truth become obvious from this perspective. By interpreting the proverb in this new way, it felt like I was speaking the truth.

But Mother probably wouldn't have liked this interpretation. She had taught me absolute sincerity. With rare exceptions, she behaved sincerely, if not with everyone, at least with me. She never bothered to hide from me her great pride and ambition, or the intensity of her discontents, her doubts, and her jealousies. She never hesitated to reveal all her truths, which I, as her daughter, was supposed to digest without difficulty. Yet she didn't accept my truths. She didn't want to believe I had truths of my own. If by some accident such truths did exist, Mother would do whatever she could to suppress them. So I came to understand that sincerity was not for everyone. Utter sincerity was the luxury of the strong.

GRANDMOTHER BELIEVES THAT LORD NILOU HAS A
list of the names of everyone alive. The names he gives
us are often different from the ones given us by our
parents. Before me, Mother had possessed other things.
She had raised birds in cages. She fed them in the morning, stroked them in the evening, walked them on Sun-
days, still in their cages, and locked them up in the
bathroom from time to time to punish them for cheeping
too much. When these birds were no longer enough to
appease her maternal longings, she sold them to the Happiness Café. Then she conceived me and named me Yan-
Zi: Swallow. I hate this bird's name. I want to know my
real name on the Lord's list. It's supposed to include all

things—presidents and thieves, pandas and rats, children and birds.

Lord Nilou doesn't succumb to laziness, or the world would be in chaos. In the morning, he gets up and scans his long list. His reading ability far surpasses that of computers. Then he takes a pencil, circles some names and crosses out others. Those circled will settle into the belly of a woman; those crossed out will die that very day. He makes equal numbers of cross-outs and circles. He arranges marriages, plans accidents, and sets important dates. For example, he wanted Chairman Mao to die exactly on September 9, 1976, not a day before or a day after. And he decided that I was to be born right when Mother's body lost a lot of liquid and not before. He sows hatred in love, trouble in peace, decline in prosperity. He announces the eternal through the ephemeral. He consoles birth through death, exchanging one life for another. That's how he maintains the equilibrium of his kingdom.

I knew all this thanks to Grandmother. You could say she had opened my third eye. And well before my death, I knew Lord Nilou was paying attention to me. I felt his pencil suspended over my skull. He followed me everywhere, his invisible presence constantly revealed to me by a vague sadness and an uncontrollable rage.

I HAD REFLECTED AT LENGTH ON THE VARIOUS METH-
ods. First I thought of jumping out the window of our
apartment. That way, I could finally get Mother to understand that I wasn't happy at home. I didn't know how
else to show her. I had never dared say so, since she was
convinced that I was unspeakably lucky to be her child.
But as we were only on the second floor, I was afraid of
blowing it. I couldn't bear the prospect of spending the
rest of my life in a wheelchair. They wouldn't have to
send me to a psychologist to punish me; Mother alone,
with her tears, her shouting, her threats, her irony, and
her pity, would make me regret my move. She would
even be happy about it, since once I was crippled I would

be utterly dependent on her. I would have a hard time getting out, even in the daytime; I wouldn't be obliged to marry, and with only spinster status I would no longer be a source of shame for the family. I would stay at home like a good girl in the good old days. I would be her daughter forever.

Everywhere the city had sprouted buildings of deathly heights, but they didn't attract me. I preferred to die near Mother. I would expire at her feet, before her eyes. She had planned my arrival; now she must witness my retreat. It would be up to her to complete the work she'd begun: to collect my body and clean the traces of my blood—my blood, which was her blood too. I wanted to see the look of horror on her face. I wanted to feel her trembling. My final image of this world would be of a mother crumbling.

FINALLY, I gave up on heights and chose the sleeping pill, a gentle, classic poison, good for tragedies. I went looking for pills during the Festival of the Moon. I went to several pharmacies to avoid suspicion. We are prisoners of life itself, not only of our bodies. You've got to know the ropes to get out. It's not enough to decide to die; you have to get the approval of others, at least of the pharmacists. But go talk to them face to face! They'd lean toward me as if I were a child, hardly able to keep from laughing. I understand, miss, they would begin. Men are pigs, they'd chuckle, they're not worth dying for . . . What's that? There is no man? Well, that's just it, you need to find one! But in the meantime, think of your parents. Do your parents have gray hair? . . . Think of their hair. In the end, with a little luck, I'd walk away with a tiny tube of crushed pearls. Here, they'd say, in a show of seriousness, this is what you need, to take better care of your pretty face.

I had to lie.

I now possessed a sufficient quantity of pills. If they were still sitting in my purse it wasn't because I was afraid to take the next step. I understood that if I did what I was about to do correctly, I wouldn't feel a thing. But the moon was full just now. We had to celebrate family unity in this season when the wind would be snatching all our heat.

THE FESTIVAL of the Moon was wonderful. We were given a half day off. By the afternoon, my two office colleagues could barely sit still. Lao-Ma was waiting for his friends to play cards—his life's passion—while Hua waited impatiently by the phone, probably hoping to call her boyfriend. The lines were all tied up: everyone was trying to reach someone else.

I was getting ready to leave the office when Chun

called. He was off too and suggested we visit his parents. I had a mother and a father. I had enough parents already. His didn't interest me. There was a long silence on the other end of the line. I could picture his pale forehead, his disgruntled look. His visit to my parents hadn't been free. He expected to be repaid. He had said his "don't you think?"s to my mother, and he was hoping I'd return the favor in kind. His family needed a daughter-in-law, any one would do, but a proper daughter-in-law, one who didn't voice her every thought or, better still, one who had no thoughts. Chun always said: Come to our house. "Our house" meant his parents' house. If I married him, I would have to go live with his parents. But that wasn't my plan.

"I have other plans," I told him, ready to hang up.

He didn't like that phrase. I shouldn't have plans without him.

"Something's going on in your head that worries me," he began.

Perhaps that was why he hadn't left me in disgust over my moods. In a tender, almost pleading, voice, he invited me to a restaurant. But missing a meal at home was out of the question. Mother attached great importance to the table ceremony, to having the members of the family eat together, each in his place, listening to the few things she had to say about them—her criticisms, that is. But I agreed to go out in the evening, after dinner of course, which spared me having to celebrate the festival at home.

I TOOK a noisy street with lots of drugstores. The flow of pedestrians pushed me along. There was a slight breeze. The leaves were falling continuously and crunched beneath people's feet. The street seemed hectic. For a month now, the moon cakes had been piling up in stores. People bought them, gave them to friends, and ate them in abundance, hoping for harmony and union. As for me, before I left this world, I wanted dried prunes. I couldn't find them, and asked a saleslady if she had any. She looked at me harshly, then quickly, disdainfully, turned to the other customers. Her hair shook a little after her head stopped moving. An old woman next to me told me not to bother her. "Look at it her way, young lady. Moon cakes are better than dried prunes, which make you think of old faces."

Indeed, the lady had so many wrinkles that her head seemed almost artificial. I thought of Grandmother. She loved moon cakes. I decided to buy some. When she handed me the box, the saleslady's features had visibly softened.

I spent the rest of the afternoon alone with Grandmother. Father was at the university at one of those gatherings to which all the faculty, even those who had retired, were invited, where they all chatted and nibbled watermelon seeds. Mother wouldn't be home until the sun had disappeared behind the red roofs. I put my purse on the table and watched Grandmother bite into a cake, her eyes pulsating with pleasure.

I wondered what the point of making round cakes was. How could they represent harmonious union when they were destined to be chewed up by teeth, pulverized in the stomach, absorbed by the flesh, and returned to the earth?

Grandmother thought we should save some cakes for Father and Mother. I told her to simply think of herself. In the home of Lord Nilou, there would be no moon cakes to eat. There would be no union to destroy. No harmony to savor.

CHUN WAITED FOR ME IN THE ALLEY. THE STARS WERE hiding, intimidated no doubt by the bold light of the moon. The sky seemed to me lonelier than ever.

Everything might have been different between us if Mother hadn't invited Chun to dinner and if he hadn't kept saying "don't you think?" We would have become good friends over time. I would have believed in his capacity to heal my unhealable sadness and to wrest me from Mother's arms, solid as handcuffs. We might even have fled and gone to live somewhere else. But he preferred to ask Mother for my hand, because before belonging to him, this ever so disobedient and tempting hand had belonged to Mother. It's for your own good, he would say in a tone strangely similar to Mother's.

We walked the deserted street. His lips trembled. I could hear him speaking vaguely of the future and reciting his favorite poem, a poem that had been adapted and worn out for centuries by the lovesick, by those nostalgic for the eternal:

. . .

It will be enough to remain in this life
For the moon to unite us from a thousand leagues.

Thus you had to live a long time, preferably forever, to overcome time and space, to unite with someone, to chain yourself to a place and melt into something. To gather the shards of the broken mirror. To have a future. But the earth was turning at top speed, scrambling everything in its wake, ripping the child from the body of its mother, cutting the chain of blood and covering over the traces of history. If, twenty-five years ago, Mother had conceived a moment earlier or a moment later, I wouldn't have been born or I wouldn't be me; someone else would be living in my place and everything would be different. But death was written in advance; Lord Nilou awaited us while the pills were screaming at me from my purse . . .

I stared into Chun's face. The moon, which seemed to become less and less perfect at every instant, shone on his forehead.

"If you want," I said to him abruptly, "let's do it now. Let's not wait. It's now or never."

He stepped away from me brusquely. Then, collecting himself, he decided to stroke my hair cautiously and scold me like a child: "Be good, my bad girl."

A moment later, he added: "Now I know why your mother can't stand you."

Still, he couldn't hide his panting. He began to list the marriage preparations in order to distract himself. I hated him right then for the condescending tone he took with me, for the way he meddled in my dealings with Mother, and even for his ill-concealed desire. I lifted his hand from my head and cast it away, walking fast. I knew he had stayed where he was, motionless and bathed in the white light. He was regretting his reaction. He spent his life regretting everything and he knew it. Things always moved faster than his thoughts. Love had fled faster than the marriage preparations. There was nothing he could do.

WHILE MY BODY WAITS OUTSIDE THE CREMATORIUM, my close relatives are treated to a tofu banquet. Grandmother clearly said that you don't celebrate a premature ending, that you give a tofu banquet only in honor of those who die old. But Mother doesn't listen to her. A generous meal should be offered to thank the guests for crying over the remains of her daughter. At the same time, she counts on proving that she loves her daughter and that the rumors of suicide are just rumors. Most people gladly accept the invitation. They are disturbed by my death: this so-called accident shattered their illusions about youth and eternity. So Mother is supposed to make it up to them, restore their peace of mind, give them back their lost gaiety, fill their stomachs in order to appease their spirits and put them back in harmony with time.

I follow them into the restaurant, which is close to the funeral home. The tables are laid with every kind of meat imaginable. Yet according to Grandmother the tofu banquet should be a vegetarian meal, a sign of respect for Lord Nilou and the creatures who have joined him in his kingdom, including the pigs and the fish. But tradition had to change as society progressed. Today it takes not just tofu to please Lord Nilou, but in particular lots of meat, many sacrificed lives.

I even smell beef just as they're pushing my body into the fire.

"It's real beef, you know," says Mother, addressing everyone.

I realize she is talking not about the meat they're in the process of tearing apart at the table, or about my astrological sign, but about me with my oxlike nature. Suddenly I have the crazy idea that I am being eaten by Mother's guests. Now I know why they have come to celebrate my death. They love flesh. My cousin proves it, saying to her brother, "Eat as much as you can, even if it's not the best tofu banquet. When my fiancé's father died, I had turtle soup! Turtles live so long, you know, that their meat isn't very tasty anymore, but it's good for your health."

She seems to envy the turtles their long lives. By eating turtle soup, she hopes the meat of the animal will grow inside her. She dreams of becoming a turtle too. But this time she has to be content with a grilled bird. She tears off a wing, dips it in sesame oil, then lifts it to her outstretched tongue. The white flesh slides down her warm throat. She spits the little pieces of bone onto the table. Finally, she closes her eyes and frowns. Maybe she sees my fleshless face again. I can hear her stomach growling. Just then black smoke rises from the chimney of the crematorium and drifts toward the restaurant. It passes through the window and envelops the table. The guests raise their heads in alarm. My cousin notices this suspicious smoke too, and makes an effort to keep the meat from traveling back up her throat. I know that my body is reduced to ash. I feel weakened. The fresh air is sucking me away. But I'm enjoying these faces, so sad and yet ravenous. If only I could stay a little longer! I cry for help. No one hears me, but Mother stands up. She's not eating. She's cold. She goes to close the window. Oh! Mother, Mother! Do you realize that it's too late, that I will never be grateful to you? I fly around the table. I'd like to tell my cousin that it's not nice to wish she had some turtle to eat at my funeral. If she wants to live as long as a turtle, she'll have to understand that it isn't enough to eat the animal, you also have to imitate it, live at its pace, be easy to please, shortsighted and moderate in appetite. But my cousin likes to eat. Her body absorbs everything in its passage. Death stalks her. She lives in haste.

PERHAPS THE person who is most alive at this moment is my father. Mother pays him no attention. He goes to sit next to my cousin. I have the impression of being crushed by the weight of time standing still in this restaurant. Father leans toward her and takes her hands. He seems intoxicated by such a fine meal, such fine company. He is preoccupied with life at this moment, which carries him beyond his thoughts about the nature of things, beyond the memory of his daughter, beyond the scrutiny of his wife, and, finally, beyond death. Suddenly, he blushes a horrible red. Saliva dribbles from his gaping mouth. When his face gets too close to my cousin's, I start to shake. The plates shake too. My cousin bursts out laughing.

Father freezes but is slow to pull back. I examine him sadly. I'd prefer not to recognize him, but I realize that this is no doubt my father's face. I must hate my father, then! Can I hate my father without hating myself? I want to get away from him for fear that the gleam on his forehead will project onto me, that his genes will stick to me and follow me all the way to Lord Nilou. But an inexplicable powerlessness keeps me from moving.

Stripped of the mask of intellection, prey to an indiscreet desire, Father's face is before me in all its animal reality. More than ever before, I should discover the nature of love, how it is that we are born and live. It knocks me out just as my cousin's breath knocks me out. I see myself falling from a cliff crowded with the living. I'd prefer to take cover in the corner now, but I can't. I'm not like them. I don't have two feet on the ground. I can't stay in one place anymore. Against my wishes, I fly above all these heads I hate so much. I circle around Mother. I'm still not free.

UPON LEAVING the restaurant, their lips shiny with grease, the guests must accompany Mother and Father home and drink a tea that will help them to digest and find consoling words. They sigh and burp into their sleeves, saying to themselves, "What a pity, a real pity." A pity that the meat had been charred or too well done, that life does not last. In front of the door, Mother makes a fire that will keep Lord Nilou out of the house—a fire that every guest must step over to surmount his own death. I feel as if shadows are beginning to leap over me. I am now completely excluded and outcast. Mother makes sweet tea for everyone. Father drinks his slowly, under Mother's anxious, don't-ask-any-questions gaze.

This is no joke. Mother is serious, she never jokes.

Everything she does in life has meaning. Right now, she is at war with Lord Nilou and with me as well. Grandmother told her that the spirits of the dead like to bring their kin with them in their lonely fall. The kin have to fight as best they can, they have to drink this sweet hot water in order to chase away the memory of the cemetery and recover a taste for life. Seeing that Father, her only surviving relative, has obeyed her command, Mother nods in satisfaction. Then she drinks a cup as well. Sugar water flows inside her body and burns her stomach. The pills would have had the same effect on me, I tell myself, if I'd had the time to swallow them.

Mother closes the front door. I stay outside. I considered haunting her house and scaring her, but I don't feel like it anymore. Deep down, I don't feel like anything anymore, ever since the fire died that burned my body and expelled my spirit. The alley is dustier than usual today.

DIRTY HANDS WAS BEING PERFORMED IN TOWN. I couldn't deny myself the pleasure of going to see this play, since it was unlikely to interfere with my decision. The tickets were distributed by the union representative. The plays chosen were often as depressing as the work at the office. But those who chose not to join in the outing had to remain at their desks, wallowing in the solitary routine, haunted by the feeling that they were being robbed, that part of their salary was being deducted every month for nothing. So we went to the theater regularly. This time, not without some hesitation, the union rep had chosen to introduce us to a work by Sartre. "That foreigner finally had the sense to write a relatively comprehensible story," she said.

Bi arrived in the afternoon. Hua called him her guy. She had managed to get him a ticket. There were always some tickets turned in by those who were out sick. I had the impression that the number of people out sick rose on these occasions. I hadn't bothered to invite Chun. Hua introduced her boyfriend to Lao-Ma and me and suggested we go to the theater together. Bi had a rugged beauty; he was strong, of medium height, with regular features. Blue veins swelled on the backs of his hands. The skin on his face seemed too worn for his age. He had wrinkles everywhere, on his neck, at the corners of his eyes and mouth . . . I yearned to stroke the wrinkles one by one with my finger. I loved men marked by time. The suggestion of death gave them a fragile power— their fleeting lives inspired a lasting tenderness in me. He spoke little, surprising me with his calm. Hadn't this obvious beauty, no doubt the object of many girls' desire, compromised his intelligence yet? Like Mother, I was prone to make snap judgments. I supposed that in order to be so wise today he must have been a homely and lonely child, and that if he managed to make his beauty last much longer he'd become less intelligent in his old age. Right now he was at his best.

Hua whispered in my ear that they were getting ready to buy furniture.

"Have you found a room?" I asked Bi.

He looked at me as if he didn't understand.

Hua had to step in: "A room for us."

"Oh, no, no, not yet."

The groom-to-be shook his head. He seemed embarrassed. I wondered if it was because of my question, his answer, or Hua's explanation.

The four of us crammed into the bus, first Lao-Ma and I, then Hua and Bi. We had trouble standing up straight. We were pushed, shoved, and crushed. We had found a window seat for Lao-Ma. Bi stood behind Hua and me. When the bus stopped and started abruptly, he made a point of supporting us by the arm. I had the crazy idea that he kept his hand on my back a few moments too long. I blushed. Lao-Ma seemed bothered to be sitting alone, a privilege normally granted old ladies.

"Yan-Zi," he said to me, standing up, "take this seat. Your face is red. It's stifling in here."

He helped me sit down on the banquette. He left me his old person's seat without realizing that by doing so the inversion of age was perhaps taking on unexpected meaning. I was still sweating. Hua handed me a paper fan. I caught Bi looking at me and turned away. I glanced out the window. He was all I could see. I saw him without looking at him. Waves of heat rose from the depths of my body. It doesn't matter, I told myself, it'll pass, it'll be the last time, I promise, the last . . .

The theater was on Liberation Street. The sky was dark, the street all but deserted. Dead leaves were being burned on the sidewalk. As we got off the bus, a handful of ashes flew in our faces, kicked up by the wind.

All through the show my eyes hurt. I couldn't understand what was happening onstage, whereas I usually guessed the whole story in the first five minutes. I noticed that the characters seemed tormented. And I cried, which was a good way to wash out my eyes.

AS WE left the theater, Bi offered to treat us to tea. He chose the Happiness Café. The proprietress seemed to know him. How was it that I hadn't met him before? We must have been in this very spot at the same moment several times without meeting. Perhaps we had watched the same street scenes through the same window. All this time we had remained strangers. Grandmother called that fate. She always wrinkled her eyebrows when she spoke of fate, because according to her fate could never be good. This was Hua's first time here and she surveyed every corner. That meant Bi had a refuge his fiancée didn't know about. Lao-Ma spoke to us about everything and nothing. I kept quiet. Bi asked if I was all right. I remarked that the days were getting shorter now. At this he began gazing at the sky. Lao-Ma said that it was because of the Festival of the Moon. After the festival, the nights always began eating the days. Hua protested: "Don't be like Yan-Zi! She spends her time lamenting the days that are dead or the ones that are going to die."

Suddenly, we heard honking. Bicycles and cars stopped in the middle of the street. Curious onlookers hurried over, suppressing their smiles. They were expecting to witness a bloody scene, an accident, or a scandal of some kind. Finally an appetizing story to serve up at dinner. They would nibble it late at night, happy and well rested. A few minutes later the waiter came back and told us about the incident: "A man on a bicycle was hit by a car. It could have happened anytime, but now the traffic is completely blocked." He says all this in a reproachful manner: reproachful of the reckless driver, of course, but perhaps also of the victim, who disturbed traffic by not dying at the right moment. He went on to serve his clients with his usual smile. The entire room heaved a sigh before reaching for another serving or another cup of tea.

Since the street was chaotic and Hua and I were a little shaken, Bi offered to accompany us home. He decided to take his fiancée first. An hour later, we found ourselves alone on Liberation Street, which, after a quick scrubbing, was elegant once again.

IN THE DAYS THAT FOLLOWED, I FELT BI'S GAZE AND
the heat of his hand on my back. I continued my comings
and goings, my bag hooked over my left shoulder, three
bottles of sleeping pills tucked inside. At meals, I would
bring up politics out of the blue, as Father used to do.
Mother was probably shocked. I didn't look at her. These
days she didn't exist. Bi had become my obsession. I saw
him all the time, everywhere. He was hiding in Hua's
eyes, on Chun's forehead, in the depths of dangerous al-
leys. I wanted to have him at all costs, to grab him with
all my might, to grip him with my fragile fingernails. I
wanted my gaze to pierce his beautiful body, so alive yet
so mortal. Only light would survive over time. And my

gaze would be a light. My desire was impatient, a dying woman's thirst.

ON SATURDAY afternoon, I found an excuse to leave the office early. I waited for him at the Happiness, without much hope. He was a virtual stranger. Someone approached, walked away, then came back again. It was probably the waiter. I hardly saw him. All my life—Mother liked this expression, so laden with time that I could finally say it myself—I had waited for someone or something I couldn't see clearly. I felt I'd spent my life drinking tea in this restaurant, waiting. Waves of voices traveled toward me. The windows across the street were teeming with colors, but all I could see was light. How I despised this pointless waiting, this desire for things other than light. I heard footsteps, the steps of Lord Nilou, no doubt. I had to hurry. I took out a piece of paper and began my letter:

"Dear Mother, I am going to die for you. I have waited for you, in the hope of changing my mind. I have waited so long. The slightest touch of your strong hand could save me. Or a little smile. You smile so rarely, Mother . . ."

THESE FEW lines left me unsatisfied. I still had a hard time imagining that Mother's face was as beautiful as a flower, or that my impending death would be an easy descent into sleep that would heal me of my chronic insomnia. My desire to disappear into this letter was in vain. I didn't have the role down. A good actor retreats into his character, which is all he needs. At that moment, Bi appeared at the door of the restaurant. And I tore up the paper.

HE WALKED right toward me, as if we had an appointment. We looked at each other. The waiter brought us tea and took away my cold cup. The silence was strangling me. I tried to say something but stopped instantly when I noticed the absurdity of my words. He smiled.

When the sunlight left the restaurant, he stammered that he was still free. He placed the accent on the word "still." Meaning that it wouldn't take much for him not to be free and that he was only free by chance. I considered that I was no freer than he was. There was Chun, there was Mother, there was Lord Nilou.

I looked outside. The street was cluttered with vehicles. He wanted to know what I was thinking. I pictured a mangled body and said, "The cars, you know . . ."

I had promised Mother I'd cook that night. I rose to go. He grabbed my arm and I lost my balance. He asked me to join him for dinner.

"I don't like going out on the street at this hour, anyway," he added.

Once again, I thought about the accident.

I went to the counter to call Mother. I knew what was waiting for me. I could already see her turning in circles, striking the empty place at the table. In such cases, I had to give rock-solid reasons: urgent work at the office or a serious illness. Mother counted the minutes of my commute. Our appointments for meals and their preparation were fixed with military precision. One day, I was invited to a dinner party. Since she knew the names and addresses of all my friends by heart, she went to check with one of them whether the gathering had actually taken place. Humiliated by her lack of trust, I pointed out that I was no longer a minor and that I had the right to choose where to eat my meals. Astounded by my reply, Mother asked Uncle Pan to judge the matter. My uncle was of the opinion that I shouldn't disappoint Mother, who had given me so much, who loved me in her way, and who asked for nothing but that I should eat with her. At these words, Mother began to cry, and I felt guilty. From then on, I always ate at home. Since we finished meals late, I missed all the eight o'clock movies.

On the telephone, Mother demanded an explanation. I had prepared a lie. I was going to tell her that on a whim I'd decided to spend some time with a girlfriend.

She didn't like other people's schemes. If something bad had to happen to her—that I should go out for the evening, for instance—Mother preferred that it should be unplanned, if not accidental. But Bi approached and took my hand. I had the impression that the hand no longer belonged to me. And my head wasn't obeying either. I forgot the rules of the game. Without trying to hide my impatience, I made the mistake of speaking brusquely: "I'll gladly give you a report later on."

Mother got worried, she wanted to know where and with whom I was at that very moment. I was afraid she'd come to get me. I cried, "But, Mother, you can't supervise me so much: I'm free, aren't I, free!"

She hung up. I felt the pulsing of her veins at the other end of the line. At the thought of the scene that awaited me at home, I had to lean against the counter a moment. I couldn't understand Bi's smile. I told him what Mother had said, and he shrugged it off: "Come on, your mother hardly said anything. She might not be happy about it, but what can she do to you? You can't please everyone."

I knew she could do far more than simply be displeased, and that if I didn't succeed in pleasing her I would never please anyone. When I was eighteen years old, a boy named Hong-Qi had left me because I couldn't please my mother.

Bi soon understood that he had underestimated

Mother. He ordered chicken for me, but all I could do was twiddle my chopsticks. I stared at this young man sitting opposite me. My head had cooled down. I wasn't blushing anymore. He still seemed seductive to me, and this made me sadder than ever. He asked me why I wasn't eating. I confessed that it was because of him.

"You're wonderful."

He was relaxed and had forgotten all about my mother.

OUT ON the street, he took my hand in his again. I let him do as he pleased. Sometimes he stopped in front of furniture store windows. He had never had his own room. It struck me that had he found a room sooner he would have bought furniture with Hua already and would now be taking her hand instead of mine.

"What's the first thing you'd do if you had a room?" I asked suddenly.

He stopped and turned toward me. His eyes pierced through me. He began walking again, in silence. Our hands had become damp. Soon, this dampness made our contact uncomfortable. I wanted to withdraw my hand but he was holding it tight.

We headed slowly toward a park. There was a long line at the gate. You had to wait for a ticket. People who didn't have their own rooms brought their sweethearts to the park. In front of us, a young couple was waiting impatiently. The man was running his hands all over the woman's body, while she stretched her neck to see if the line had gotten any shorter. The bodies in front of us were intertwined. When we reached the counter, Bi left me to pay for the tickets. We plunged into a darkness that called for an intimacy we didn't yet possess. The slightest brushing of our bodies made us jump. He didn't take my hand again. I felt as if my hands were abandoned, idle and superfluous. I slid them into my pockets.

BI WAS PHILOSOPHIZING AS MUCH AS HE COULD. HE
was trying to imprison my soul in his spirit. He must
have done the same thing with Hua and all the other
girls he'd met. I vaguely heard him say that life was not
worth living but that the smartest and the stupidest continued to live on. I figured that I was very stupid because,
at that moment, all I wanted was for him to take my
hand again. He didn't, which made me sad. I would have
liked to make the first move, to put my arms around his
neck, for example, but Mother always said that a girl
must never act loose or appear easy. Since men could be
loose, it was a girl's duty to give them solidity, to control
them with a gentle coolness, to maintain the gravity of

things, to live like mountains. Mother had known more men than I and no doubt understood them better. I was thinking, nonetheless, that if this man took my hand again, I would take advantage of his looseness. We wouldn't have a second chance, and I knew it. I wouldn't have a second chance.

He chose a bench lit by the generic kind of lamppost found on every street in the city.

"Light makes people reasonable," he said.

"But why bother?"

I hated this ashen light, which clung to my cheeks and made me look like my father. This man next to me was pretending not to understand me. Sometimes, the black leaves quivered in the bushes behind our bench. The murmurs and sighs grew louder, broken by laughter and muffled cries. We even heard a little slapping against bare skin. This nocturnal recital seemed to tie his tongue: he stopped talking. He didn't move. Silence accumulated between us like a storm cloud in a summer sky.

Finally the bushes grew quiet again. It was time to go home. We dragged our feet toward the gate.

I didn't look at him. But my spirit soaked him up. His body was shifting every which way in my head. He must have felt it, because poor Bi was hardly breathing. I wouldn't let him go. It would be tonight or never. But he could wait. He would patiently follow the steps. He would obtain his marriage certificate. He would sleep with Hua or someone else in his well-furnished room. He could afford to act with modesty and restraint, because he would live a long time. He would live a long time by dint of saving his energy. But I didn't have time. Mother was mad. She was expecting me at home. My judgment awaited me. The punishment would be harsh. I had to live then and there, that very instant. Quick, not a minute to lose. I had to exhaust myself to the last breath or it would be too late. A girl kept skin on her bones by nourishing herself on patience, Mother had said, which would help her preserve her worth as long as possible, especially in the eyes of men. This principle of economy—this avarice of desire, this strategy of possession—was useless to me now. My bones weighed so little I couldn't feel my body. I could already see myself reduced to ashes. There was no doubt about it. I was worth nothing at all.

"What if this were the last time we saw each other?" I asked him, holding back a sob.

"No way!" he protested.

"But if something were to happen . . ."

"Whatever happens, we'll see each other again!"

"But it'll be different," I cried. "It won't be like tonight."

He stopped. He stared at me like a stranger and grabbed me roughly by the arm. He hurt me; I wondered if it was out of desire or despair. We returned toward the darkness hurriedly, passing people heading for the gate. One of them winked at us: "Lose something in the grass?"

I HAD a great sense of relief as we emerged from the bushes. Bi stayed close to me. The deed was done. My body had been torn apart. Mother had hatched a body that was no longer worth anything. This body, now impure, would mix more easily with the muck. Calmly, I arranged my hair and the collar of my shirt. This was the first time. I was twenty-five years old and this was the first time. I felt I had gotten revenge against everyone for my lost youth. I had gotten revenge against Mother, who had brought me into the world without telling me all the truths about life—she who had married at eighteen wanted me to remain a virgin as long as possible and would throw herself in the river upon learning what had happened tonight. I had gotten revenge against Chun, who was so worried about compromising my good-girl status that he hadn't dared to touch me. He would allow himself to do so only after having put his signature on some forms, shaken the hands of strangers at a banquet, and lit some colored firecrackers that would make the air reek. He was like my father, my professor-father from before the accident: his mind was stronger than his body. At the same time, I had gotten revenge against my father of days past who had such contempt for the Sunday morning market, full of vegetables and meat, blood and earth, all those petty things he called carnal. If Mother were to ask me her favorite question again, if she were to ask me whether fire could be hidden behind paper, I'd tell her no, fire couldn't be hidden behind paper, in fact, and it was better to do away with the paper.

And yet I hadn't really learned anything that night. It was painful. I was too old to do it for the first time. If I could have made my debut at eighteen, like Mother, I thought, I wouldn't have had to suffer so much. It must be marvelous when the body is young and supple. Alas, I'd never be eighteen again. Time passed at its own speed, unwavering, with no thought of repaying me for my virginity. Because of Mother, my life would always be flawed. And it had all happened too quickly between Bi and me. That too was because of Mother. I had swallowed a truth that had quickly gotten lost in my belly. I was looking for it inside myself, but all I found was a vague hollow.

On the street, I kept on stroking Bi's back. Now that his enthusiasm had melted in the park bushes, his body was soft and disgusting. He put his hand on my shoulder out of exhaustion. I pointed to the sky streaming with white light and he raised his head to be polite. He didn't stop when we passed in front of the furniture store. I thought of Hua: "What will she do if she finds out?"

"She'll find out sooner or later," he replied without hesitation.

"She loves you."

"If she could love me, she'll love someone else just as well."

I was shaken by this reasoning, whose stark lucidity brought to mind the premature wrinkles on his face. Deep down, I wasn't all that different from Hua, no one was really different from anyone else; death made us universal. And Bi was smart enough to understand that. After a few moments I began again: "You'd better forget me."

"Who do you think I am? I'm not that irresponsible!"

So now I had become his responsibility. I was no longer a virgin after tonight and he felt he was to blame. He was committing himself to staying with me from now on in the name of a truth that had already disappeared inside my body.

I asked him if I too should feel responsible for him. He said no, that it was really his fault. I felt like laughing, but I didn't. I knew that my laughter would scare him. I tried to reassure him—it was no one's fault, I was happy about what I had done. He thanked me for my generosity but still thought it was his fault. Now I became impatient; abandoning my polite demeanor, I opened my mouth wide, revealing my irregular teeth, and shouted the way Mother did at me: "Then I pardon your crime!"

He took his hand off my shoulder and looked at me, worried.

The street had become as calm as a cemetery. The night wind swept the dead leaves. I was cold. I was waiting for him to forget his misdeed and remember the tenderness we had had for each other. I was waiting for him to say to me: I'll never leave you because I love you more than anyone else. I was looking, without knowing it and perhaps without wanting to admit it, for something stronger than death, something as absolute as light, something that could keep me a little longer in this life. With my soul already out in the sea of the void, my body was still seeking to cling somewhere. For me, Bi was a branch floating on the surface of the water. I was counting on him. His face was so richly engraved, his body so strong and his shoulders so restful. He could make me forget Mother and throw away my pills. But he wasn't thinking of me. He was only thinking of his responsibility. He didn't want to save me. Or he couldn't.

He walked me home. A menacing light shone from the window. Mother wasn't in bed. On the doorstep, I thanked him for the evening, by virtue of which I would be able to die with my heart unburdened and my body worthless. I could hardly see his face. I felt as if I were speaking alone in the darkness. He pinched my hands gently as if to wake me. How confused he must have looked. I explained that I hadn't wanted to die without doing it once. He seemed reassured, and swore, coolly but with great elegance, that he didn't want to die after what we had done.

As he walked away, I was trying to remember whether he wore glasses. All I knew was that he was my colleague's fiancé, that his name was Bi, and that he liked furniture.

I PUSHED OPEN THE DOOR. MOTHER WAS WAITING FOR
me near the window that overlooked the alley. I started
at the sight of her disheveled face. A long strand of gray
hair fell to her pale lips. Her eyes shone strangely. I
recalled the day she had said to me angrily, "Watch it!
If you keep disappointing me, I'll lose my patience and
my reason. And if I lose my reason, if my brain becomes
sick like your father's, I won't hesitate to beat you to
death!" I had been terrified and dreamed several times
of a gruesome scene: I was lying in a pool of blood, my
throat slit, at the foot of my parents' bed; Father was
sitting on the bed, trembling, the still-warm knife in his
hand; Mother had opened the door for the neighbors and

was explaining that it was just an unfortunate accident. People believed her because she couldn't stop sobbing.

I'd have to act quickly if I wanted to die a decent death. I didn't know whether to pull out my pills or pounce on Mother. I was ready to poison myself or to strangle her. This had to end, one way or another. My life had to be stopped and the shame erased. The shame of having a Mother and of being me, the shame that I had lived and was obliged to keep going. I recoiled without realizing it, out of habit no doubt; pulling away had always been my most natural reflex when it came to Mother. In the same way, twenty-five years earlier, I had hung back in her womb, I hadn't wanted to come out. And now the time had come to return to the void, and I was still pulling back. I didn't know where to go, where to stand.

She studied me for a second, then charged at me: "You dare return to this house! Go back to your men."

I headed slowly for the door; she grabbed me by the hair and pushed me against the wall. "Wait! Before you go, tell me how many men would be enough for you!"

A shadow emerged from the hallway. It was Father, a glass of water in his hand. "She's a . . . an idiot!" he said, panting, his eyelids red.

"I take after you, Father."

His glass flew at me and broke with a hollow sound on the floor. Cold water trickled down my chest. A few wet hairs stuck to my cheeks. We stared at each other in silence. His gaze ordered me to lower my eyes, but I didn't. I was busy staring at him. I thought to myself, here he is, my father, whose genes I carry. I didn't want to carry this man's genes anymore, and I was going to kill them by killing myself. My murderous look irritated him. I followed the movement of his hand as he raised it high. Good, that's right, yes, hard, really hard, finish the job, hurry up, don't wait, finish me off now, once and for all. Lightning finally struck my skull. No, that's not enough, Father dear, that was too soft, too ineffectual, too human. I forced myself to remain standing. I looked steadily in his direction, but all I could see was a living shadow. "Again," I screamed, "again!" As in a dream, I heard Mother telling him that I was already dead as far as they were concerned, that it wasn't worth it to strike me anymore and risk going to jail. Father seemed to agree on this point and went away without a sound. Yet he would never have gone to jail. On the contrary, they would appreciate his efforts to make a good citizen of this child who exhibited such a disturbing lack of wisdom and respect. Mother's caution was baseless. Father could keep striking me without getting into any trouble.

"I did it!" I told Mother breathlessly when she turned back to me. "It was great."

"I know you went out with someone else," she said, her hands flexed and her eyes turned away.

She wouldn't look at me. She refused to understand. I wanted to know. I wanted her head, her head of stone, to be struck by lightning like mine. So I told her: "I slept with someone."

I surprised even myself by the calm of my voice and the fierce joy I felt upon uttering this statement. Mother staggered and sat on the floor.

"You did?" she murmured, breathing deeply. "How long have you known him?"

"A week."

"Ahhh! . . . Do you have feelings for each other?"

"As much as you and Father, I think."

". . . He'll marry you?"

"Of course not."

"Then why did you do it? Why?"

"For you, Mother, for you." I looked at her with amusement. She began pulling out her hair. I shut up. I mustn't push her to madness. Better that she hold on to her reason for the big moment. That way she would suffer my departure lucidly. Her every nerve would be touched by the event. She didn't know what awaited her, poor Mother. Why hadn't I told her all this earlier, she asked, all this which concerned her so very much? I repeated that I thought it was great. But I didn't say that, except for the memory of a sharp pain, I had completely forgotten the taste of the adventure and that, as I had abandoned myself to the arms of a stranger, I had been thinking only of her.

She began telling me of the suffering she had endured at my birth, the sacrifices she had made to raise me, and, finally, the hope she had placed in me. She had dreamed of a marvelous future for the two of us. In her dream, there would be a place for Father, whom we had to accept out of charity, and another for my future husband, who was necessary for the continuation of our family. I would be her chosen one. True, they had fed me on cheap vegetables for many long years, but there were good reasons for that. They had to economize in order to ensure our future, and how else to form my character but through hardship?

"You were pretty good until now," she concluded in a tone of exceptional generosity, a tone often employed, before closing the coffin, to pronounce final judgment over the departed. "You never complained, you were happy with simple food and worn clothes, you did well in school, and until now I was almost proud of you . . ."

She stopped to stifle a sob. Her eyes had turned all red. I was comforted by the effect I'd obtained. She went on: "But I didn't expect you to stoop so low, to lose yourself to men, to abandon your future, your fine future, to the hands of men. You're impatient. You expect too much from life, and you'll get nothing. No worthy man will marry you, you'll see. Your chance for happiness has gone the way of your morals. You'll spend the rest of your life without a husband, without a child, without a family, and that means without a destiny . . . The roads are blocked in front of you, and in front of me too, a black hole has opened up, we're surrounded by emptiness, and you come to me smiling and say, 'That's it, I did it!' Yes, you've done it. You've sealed your death, my poor girl. You'll live like a dead girl. My heart is dead too . . . It's partly my own fault, of course. If only I had paid more attention to those hypocrites around you, or supervised you more closely on your dates. I should have guessed at your unfortunate tendencies . . . Now the neighbors will laugh at us and spit on our backs. My life is a failure—you've destroyed me, you've destroyed everything. Are you satisfied at last? You've hurt me enough all these years, but tonight takes the prize."

"Is that it?" I asked.

"That's it."

Tears rolled down her cheeks.

A strong feeling of deliverance rocked through me. In that case, I told her, I could no longer live at home.

"Do what you want." She sighed, heading toward her room. "I won't stop you."

I LAY DOWN ON MY BED, ARMS AND LEGS SPREAD. FOR
my death, I would choose this position, a position that
would no doubt scandalize Mother. Such an unladylike
position, such abandon, such insolence. What a harlot!
Nothing like her mother. So cheap, so reckless, so common . . . Listen, think about the fact that you don't have
to live with your parents anymore. Their lives are not
your concern. You don't belong to anyone anymore. Not
to anyone. You're alone, absolutely alone. Your hands are
free, your feet are free, your head is free, you're free as
the wind. You come from nowhere and you're going nowhere. You move in space and out of space, in time and
out of time. You skirt alongside history but you have no

history. All because you don't have parents anymore. How many times has Hua complained about her family. Her father opened her letters. Her brother read her diary aloud at dinner. On her first date with Bi her mother followed them to the park to see if he was handsome enough for her daughter. Fortunately, he's not too ugly, Hua had said, which in the eyes of her parents made up for his inability to find a room.

Wouldn't it be wonderful not to have parents, then, to live far from the obligations imposed by the bonds of blood? At the thought of my room, however, a great anxiety pinched my stomach. I didn't want to die on the street. I wanted to leave my parents but not the comforts of home. I needed a private place to finish myself off in dignity. The wind was knocking at the windows. Night was yawning outside. This room was going to spit me out after having held me for so many years. I had been kept in its belly, undigested and subject to its every whim. Now that I was free—yet unable to reclaim my life, which had already been spent in countless efforts to please Mother—I was hoping at least to die a full death. It wouldn't be easy. I could already imagine the curious onlookers. The evil tongues were ready to pounce, to wag at me and slander me. I could hear the autumn winds announcing winter. And already I missed the warmth of this room. I hesitated. No, I hadn't forgotten my goal, I was not unaware of my destiny. I was conscious of a sudden fatigue. And I allowed myself to feel a little fear, the better to conquer it.

I was on the verge of opening up to Mother. But what could I tell her? That she had suffered to bring me into the world in vain, that I no longer had the slightest desire to live this life? That she should forgive my irresponsibility toward my filial duties, since I had never wanted to be her daughter to begin with? That pills were waiting patiently in my purse to bring our relationship to an end, to close this chapter filled with false hopes and disappointment? That I would rather have died in her womb than left her in such a season? That I would rather perish at her feet than go elsewhere and deliver myself to the eyes of strangers? I held myself back. You don't talk that way to the enemy before an attack. You prepare your assault in fear and solitude. Sleep would be the best solution. But even though I was awfully tempted, I couldn't swallow my pills in Mother's home. I wanted my death to attract Mother's attention, but not the police. I would make Mother suffer, of course, but sending her to prison was out of the question. She should be trapped by her daughter, locked in her death. I wasn't aiming to get at her body. Physical suffering for her was enriching and would only serve to relieve her of remorse and despair. I decided to die in Mother's presence, but not at home.

Besides, would Mother let me stay at home anymore,

even if I begged her? In the past, each time I sought liberation, she threatened to hang herself. But this time it was different. I wasn't a virgin anymore. Not being a virgin was a serious situation. Not only my body but my entire life seemed damaged. And a life destroyed was worse than nothingness. My existence was worth less than zero, since Mother would always be ashamed of me. And keeping me at home was risky; if I had dared to act so imprudently before marriage, I would certainly be capable of doing plenty of other stupid things. I was the cancer of the family.

LORD NILOU ISN'T HERE. HE SHOULD HAVE COME TO me, jotted something in his notebook, and led me to his kingdom. There I would meet generations of the formerly living awaiting their return to the world. Angry rats would bite at my shadow. Nostalgic ancestors would haunt me. Mother's parents would sigh at the sight of me. They would still be holding the bamboo ruler they used to hit Mother when she was a child, so that she would learn to be submissive yet assertive when need be. Children have to understand that true force is acquired in humility, they would say, pointing the ruler at me. Glory is impossible without discipline and the true life is always elsewhere. Kong-Zi would shake his head wearily: "Women and the mediocre are the hardest to treat." Lao-Tsu would close his eyes: "He who confronts, snaps." At these words, a crowd of young women would begin weeping in unison. Tired of quarreling with their parents, they had decided to jump in the water. In their presence, one could still smell the stench of the river that poisons our city. At this point, exasperated, Nietzsche would shout at them: "Why so limp, eh? Aren't you my sisters? You want me to whip you? Don't you want to join me in victory? Become hard, harder than your mothers, so that you can create someday, so that you can become mothers!"

We can't win because we don't know what we will become. I shall have to wait my turn to penetrate a body, any body, the body of a woman, a pig or a fly, depending on Lord Nilou's mood. He will be in charge of me, this tyrant of the Yin universe, a second mother who this time will make my death unbearable. He makes sure that we're born and die, and then that we're born again and die again, as insects, as anything. He'll do what Mother will no longer be able to do: discipline and punish me, sending me into the world of domestic animals to imbue me with greater wisdom.

But he still hasn't turned up. The kingdom of the dead seems less organized than Grandmother thinks. I don't know where to go anymore. I'm becoming nervous, because Grandmother says one must always go somewhere.

THROUGH THE fog I see a red cloud floating in the distance. I can't quite place it. It might be a wave of dust rolling in Mother's world. The dust is so thick it seems it could bury the tide of pedestrians on the street. Among this crowd, black ribbons rise and fall along with a few white flowers. This refreshes my memory. It reminds me of something funereal. Indeed, Mother and Father walk side by side, prodded by my uncles, aunts, and cousins. They're dressed in black and white. Soon this procession is drowned in a red light. Flags, plastic stars, and scarves invade the street. Suddenly I realize it's the national holiday. I had lost track of time. I had almost forgotten an unforgettable holiday. The days, the seasons, and the years are so empty that this holiday seems important. Anything can happen on this day. While on television the leaders read speeches on the future of the nation and the correctness of the path the people have traveled, we follow our own paths, eat to our hearts' content, sign contracts, marry, make love, kill. Blood flows freely when bodies are at rest. The hospitals, cemeteries, and prisons are as full as the restaurants and stores.

On this day more than any other, people live. And are happy.

Mother's eyes are red and her lips pale. Her lips swell while her pupils contract. Then her lips begin devouring the flags one by one. Mother's world has become a colorless cloud . . . I can hardly see.

SHE HAD A HABIT OF HOLDING MY HAND WHEN WE crossed the street. She grasped this living hand whole, as if it were her wallet. You have to be careful, she would say, there are so many accidents every year. When I grew taller than she was, I began to feel embarrassed and tried to withdraw my hand and move away from her. I struggled against the soft, firm restraint she exercised over me. I want you to be happy, you know, she would say.

On the occasion of family reunions, she also held my hand by force. She wouldn't look at me. The pinch of her lips told me: Don't try to escape me, daughter. People would come up to us and say the expected things:

"Your daughter has grown," one of Mother's cousins remarked.

"She looks a lot like you," added one of her nieces.

"We're old, we count on our children," sighed one of her aunts.

These compliments caused Mother to drop her facade; her face radiated pride. A rare smile peeped out of the corner of her eyes. I thought I could even hear a little laugh burst in her head. Her fingers pressed tight against my palm. I was afraid her hard nails would rip my skin and become embedded in my flesh. I anticipated the pain of the wound. I was very uncomfortable, but I didn't dare withdraw my hand. The slightest gesture risked putting her on the alert. I could live in peace so long as she basked in the satisfaction of motherhood.

I was not unaware of the place I had occupied in Mother's womb, or of what I represented to her. When we were together and had nothing to say to each other, she would take my hand and place it on the right side of her stomach: "You're here." She spoke this phrase in the present, as if I had never left her body. "How can I stop worrying about you?" she would add. "You're a piece of my flesh."

Chun had said similar things to me. When he was at the peak of passion and felt his body all hot, he often murmured: "I love you so much I feel like swallowing you whole." Or else: "I'm your big wolf, you're my little rabbit, don't ever think of escaping, you belong to me, do you hear, you belong to me, to me alone . . ." This explained Mother's eternal hatred of boys. She saw them as threatening rivals, thieves who might eat her daughter, strangers who may not even have existed way back when I was drinking Mother's blood in her belly.

I realized that my love stories were detours from the path I had taken upon leaving Mother's body. Before bringing me into the world, Mother had specific ideas concerning my future. It's for your own good, she repeated whenever she tried to convince me of them. My life was hers. I should live only through her. She sought to incarnate herself in me for fear of dying. I was responsible for carrying within me the spirit of my mother, whose body would rot sooner or later. I was supposed to become the most exact possible replica of my mother. I was her daughter.

So I had to destroy this replica at all costs. I had to kill her daughter. There was no other way of taming her. There was no other way for me to be me.

SOMETIMES I WONDERED WHETHER THERE MIGHT NOT be a compromise between life and death. I thought, for example, of leaving the city and never returning. An unexplained disappearance would hurt Mother as much as a voluntary death. An unfulfilled hope would be crueler than despair.

But would I be capable of living without her? What would I become if I were no longer her daughter? If I moved elsewhere, my new neighbors would ask me where I was from and why I hadn't stayed there. And my new friends would want to know who my parents were. They would find it strange if I told them I had no parents. Everyone had to have a mother and a father and

I would have to tell them about my own. You couldn't come into the world alone. You couldn't exist without parents. A person without parents is miserable, like a people without a history. In order for others to evaluate us easily and treat us fairly, we had to prove our roots.

You don't live only for yourself and by yourself, Mother would say to me. I've told you again and again that it's necessary, in all circumstances, to think about others first. Don't you remember what Kong-Zi said about the relationship between water and the boat? The boat rises when the water rises, the boat drops when the water drops, the boat turns over when the water splashes, the boat doesn't move when the water is dead. Did you understand all that?

Of course I understood. Mother was the all-powerful water and I was the slave of a boat. I sailed on rough waters, escape was impossible without the risk of drowning like an idiot. I would do better to stay in the water, try to study its moods and adapt as best I could.

But maybe I had never really wanted to get away. How many times, on out-of-town trips, beneath foreign-smelling sheets, had I thought of Mother's odor. She sweated when she was angry. She smelled like the black river that passed through the city. Mother told me it was also *my* river. Each time I returned home, my heart raced as I passed my river. The stench of the water wafted up from afar. It led me to Mother, just as Lord

Nilou, perhaps, led his chosen ones to his kingdom. I sought Mother in the air and she was present everywhere. She possessed me without being present. I did not have that pleasant feeling of going home. I felt more like a visitor there than anywhere else. You're a ship, Mother reproached me, your soul is never at peace and you wear me out. And indeed, over the years, I had cultivated a nautical spirit. In hallucinatory moments, I saw nothing but water. The whole world seemed to be built on liquid matter flowing in every direction. And this city, far from being a restful port, was a sea that pursued me constantly. A sea without a shore. As long as I lived, I couldn't get away from it. It had soaked through me to the bone. Its odor haunted me in my sleep. I couldn't stand the thought that with time it would become indifferent to my absence. I would have liked, before plunging into its whirlpool, to penetrate its heartless soul with my ship's fury.

I AWOKE AT THE USUAL TIME. I WASHED CAREFULLY.
I ate a bowl of rice soup with salted radishes. In the dark
corridor leading to the toilet, Mother and I crossed paths.
She jumped. Her eyelids were swollen and her back a
little hunched. She had probably slept badly too.

"Mother, you were frightened."

"Of what? What on earth should I be frightened of?"

She looked me in the eye. Did she feel anything?

I left the house right away. I took the bus that brought
me to the office every morning. I wasn't even late.

• • •

I THOUGHT about pouring the pills into my empty stomach and calling Mother later. I would have just enough time to tell her, coldly, that I loved her in spite of it all, that I was dying for her sake. She would see me taken away in an ambulance. She wouldn't have time to beg me to stay. I would have the pleasure of seeing her writhe with remorse, to note how ugly her face was, invaded by madness. Then I would smile. Yes, I would have the last laugh.

But now, my colleagues were all around me. Lao-Ma looked at me with pity from afar. Hua hurled insults at me that I could hardly understand.

Of course, Bi had spoken to her about our night together and she was upset. I tried to reassure her: "What's wrong, sweetie? You didn't lose anything, he's yours."

She restrained herself a few seconds, then burst out again: "It's too late. He's changed. He has no heart anymore, that's what he told me. You ate his heart, you . . ."

Her face was almost transformed by fury. People looked at her with curiosity. My voice grew tender: "Listen, I didn't want to hurt you. I only borrowed your man. I had to sleep with someone. I've never slept with a man, can you imagine? My fiancé doesn't want to do it before marriage, but I can't wait. You have to understand, Hua, I'm in a rush. I barely had time to do it once. I really don't have enough time to worry about hearts. Now that it's done, I don't want to see him again, I swear. You understand a little, don't you?"

She didn't understand. She fell to her knees and began crying and pounding the floor. Lao-Ma circled around us:

"Calm down, girls, calm down!"

Those who came to witness the scene thought I was immoral, if not sick. They all thought that I couldn't work that day. Maybe I'd never work again. They sent me to the office of the director, who was in charge of my moral education. I was not unaware of the possible consequences of his sermon. I could be sent to the hospital and locked up with the lunatics if the director thought it necessary. So I tried to play dumb like a little girl, to affect a voice all fragile and innocent, to gaze softly upon him as if to say: I need you, save me. The director had a daughter my age whom I reminded him of. He heaved a sigh and sank into his chair. At that point I was sure it would work out for me. But beforehand I had to confess to him, in detail, what I had done with Bi and what I had said to Hua earlier. He ended up convinced I was a victim of cultural pollution.

"You're too young," he said. "Too young! When you're young, you're particularly vulnerable to bad influences, to foreign things that sully our morals, which used to be so pure. That's why our young people need guidance at all times and in all areas . . . And most of all," he continued, "if you still had a grain of common sense, you wouldn't say in public things that simply aren't said."

"I know that, sir, but I didn't have time."

"Why are you in such a rush?"

He asked this question rhetorically, not expecting an answer. He suggested that I concentrate on my work and avoid questionable publications. He even advised me, with a complicitous wink I found distasteful, to get married as soon as possible. And to top it all off, he ordered me to go home and write a self-criticism. Generally, a really good self-criticism took at least two pages and a whole afternoon. After that I could come back to work.

Since I didn't budge right away, the director asked me what I was thinking about.

"I'm thinking of my mother."

This confession pleased him no end.

"Ah, you still love your mother. That means you're not hopeless. Your soul can still be saved. I'd like to talk to your mother. I need her cooperation. Is she strict with you?"

"Very, sir."

"Good," he said joyfully, with a slap on his desk. "In that case, I think you still have a chance. A good chance!"

The director dismissed me in good humor. I left the building under the withering stares of my colleagues. I forgot for a moment what I was doing in this place, which had become almost unrecognizable. I hadn't touched my pills. No need to call Mother, now that I was being sent back to her. Still intact, my body was on the usual bus once again. Indeed, my life was like this eternal back and forth.

AT NOONTIME, UNCLE PAN KNOCKED ON OUR DOOR. HE
often came to our house when he had work in the city.
On these occasions, I had to let him take my room and
sleep with my parents. We had a spare bed that we set
up and dismantled as necessary. From sleeping on this
shaky bed from time to time, I came to feel like a tem-
porarily placed child, a migrant in Mother's life.

Lately he'd been coming for checkups. He had stomach
cancer but didn't know. Everyone lied to him, betrayed
him. It was part of the treatment. Mother said under the
circumstances it wasn't a sin to lie, since it could help
keep my uncle alive and make him happy. To my mind,
he wasn't happy anyway—he had too many worries. He

was a skilled engineer. He drew up perfectly good plans, which his supervisors often rejected. He saw his plans as a matter of life and death. At meals, he ate very little because of his poor digestion. But he talked nonstop about his work and flew into a rage at the thought that his son had gotten bad grades in school that year. "Young people today!" he would exclaim, prompting Mother to glance at me triumphantly. So Uncle Pan worried about many things, expending his energy as if he had an eternity ahead of him.

He was sitting with his back to the window. He grew very pale toward the end of the meal, with the cruel autumn light reflecting off him. He couldn't finish his bowl of rice—which made his suffering even worse. He stared into the bowl in despair, persisted in placing one last grain of rice in his mouth. More than once he had to cover his mouth to keep back the nausea. The rest of us were done; we were waiting for him to finish in order to clear the table. Mother had to go back to work in the afternoon. She suggested that he finish later. So he put his bowl aside, his heart aching and his forehead beaded with sweat.

Mother and Uncle did this because they shared the conviction, no doubt inherited from their parents, that if one wished to obey the wishes of the sky, one must absolutely never leave a single grain of rice in one's bowl at the end of a meal. You'd be struck by lightning if you did. But first you'd be struck by your parents. When I began using chopsticks, I was made to go without supper several times for having left a little rice at the bottom of my bowl. If you had lived through the hard times as your grandparents did, Mother would say, you would understand that waste is a crime. It was only right to teach children the hardships and habits of their parents. That was how traditions were maintained from one generation to the next, and how a people survived the trials of time. Now, after twenty years of practice, I could empty my bowl with my chopsticks so that the bowl looked to have been licked clean. I now could see at a glance the slightest grain of rice at the bottom. And the bowls of leftovers scattered on the tables at the Happiness Café always made me uneasy. So I guessed that, like me, Uncle Pan had probably been punished as a child for his table habits. His parents' teachings were etched in his mind so clearly that if asked to choose between jumping out the window or leaving rice in his bowl, he would have had to think it over.

Before leaving the table, Mother told her brother that the city climate suited him better and he could stay at our house as long as he liked. What she meant was that he could entrust us with the rest of his life. No, it was nothing, what else was family for? We're here to care for you; to tend to your future, perhaps, but especially your illness, and your corpse. Uncle Pan didn't know that

Mother's generosity was conditional and that his stay at our house would be quite brief.

"But my poor niece will be forced to sleep in your room," he said with concern. "That'll become inconvenient over time. She's a big girl now."

"No, no," Mother hastened to say, shaking her head, "don't worry. Her wings have hardened, she's going to fly away."

"What do you mean, fly away? Where?"

His face came to life a little at the shock, since he knew very well I had no marriage plans as yet, and a girl never acquired wings outside of marriage.

"I found a place near my office," I said casually.

"Ah, I don't understand things anymore," he said, wiping his hand across his forehead. "It's not because of me, I hope?"

"Not at all, Uncle. Don't worry. I've been waiting for this day for a long time. I emptied the closets this morning, in fact, and you can put your things away."

He turned to Mother and declared that he had always appreciated his niece—at times he considered her extraordinary.

WHILE UNCLE drank tea with Mother, I went to pack my suitcase. I contemplated this room where I had lived for so long. As in the middle of a windswept desert, the traces of my life would swiftly be erased. Soon the closet would be filled with my uncle's clothes, arranged differently from mine. The bed would be full of the odor of another body. The imperturbable four walls which had swallowed my youth would begin to absorb what was left of another life. And when my uncle disappeared, his traces too would be cleared away. Another life would fill this room with its own habits, its lies and truths; whether healthy or sick, happy or unhappy, that life as well would end in the same bricklike coldness. The thought of this made me wish I hadn't locked myself in here so often in the past, hadn't tried to do the impossible: to please Father without becoming just like him; to sincerely love Chun without seeming to love him in front of Mother; to please Mother while disobeying her; to comfort Grandmother without irritating Mother; and to show my gratitude to my parents without appreciating the life they had given me. I wished I hadn't thought so much about so many things. People who think don't live very long, Grandmother would say. She didn't need to think to know the danger of thought. In my case, it was by thinking that I had come to understand that one mustn't think. Such disastrous habits of mind could only come from my father's genes.

I was furious at Mother for abandoning me just like that, as if it were no big deal. Of course, she was under no obligation to keep a disappointing child in her midst.

"Had I known you before you were born," she would say, "I would have had an abortion!" Nonetheless, I lingered in my room. Everything had become precious to me: the bed, the closet, the little table and metal chair. The walls hadn't been repainted since my childhood. From time to time, the white paint chipped off and the exposed parts of the walls formed interesting shapes. They were more beautiful than those paintings people called art, hung on the walls of galleries, bravely exhibited to the public. They reminded you of those serious neckties men wore. The afternoon sun came in through the window and crouched in a corner. Its discreet beauty and tender presence on the wall had always given me pleasure. I didn't think I could find it elsewhere. The sun in Mother's house would never be the same as in other people's houses. I had lost my sun. Deep down, I had never had it. What I thought to be the sun was just a reflection of a distant star, a false light, an illusion. Right then I felt the silly melancholy of farewells. I was approaching the end of a story without a beginning. This room was abandoning me too, taking with it the few things that life apparently held in store.

THEY'VE ALL GATHERED AT THE CEMETERY TO PAY
their last respects. My aunts are holding Mother's arms
for fear she'll faint—a needless precaution; Mother walks
with the steadiest step in the world. She even takes
charge of maintaining order during the ceremony. She
holds back her sobs and her tears. She refuses all consolation. For her, the death of her daughter is more a
personal failure than a sentimental loss. She accepts no
pity, especially not from her sisters-in-law, hypocrites
who would laugh at her misfortune. Yes, she knows human nature too well to give in to her feelings in such a
critical situation.

They pass one by one in front of the box containing

my body's ashes. They stare into the emptiness and cry. Those who were close to me suspect the reason for my death. Some have a guilty conscience. Uncle Pan doesn't dare admit to everyone that he was living at our house before the accident, believing I left the house in part because of him. Bi is still punishing himself for having done the improper thing with me—abandoning Hua, who has shown up as well. My colleagues, Lao-Ma among them, blame Hua for assaulting me with insults that turned out to be fatal. As for Chun, he nearly turned himself over to the police and admitted to being, in a way, my assassin. They gladly bow before this box of ashes. It's easy to abase yourself in front of nothing. They grant themselves the pathetic pleasure of humbling themselves a bit when somebody else's body vanishes— the superiority of being alive merits these few seconds of humility toward the dead. But there are limits to everything. One has to save face before the living. Thus, upon emerging from the cemetery, they all dry their eyes, recover their composure, and greet each other politely.

Mother leaves last, not because the ashes of my body are of interest to her, but because she still has a few things to say to me, an old score to settle.

"I prefer you this way," she begins in a whisper. "Yes, I prefer you in powder. You're very sweet like this, very cute, no thorns or rough spots. Your silence today is more authentic than ever. It doesn't scare me anymore—on the contrary, it's comforting. You thought you were going to drive your mother insane with your death, my poor idiot, and you might have been right, but your silence is enough to calm me now, to save me from the distress you wanted to push me to. Your final insult went the way of your body. You see, you were wrong. You were fatally wrong. You're paying too dearly for your mistake, poor girl. Books didn't make you more intelligent, naturally. How many times have I told you and your father that you have to take books in moderation, like alcohol? They perturb the spirit and harden the heart. But no one believes me. Read too much, and you confuse black and white, you take your friends for enemies, you trample the people who are dear to you. I spent my entire life trying to keep you with me, to spare you the scars of life, to prepare a future for you—as well as for myself and our family. But you left us anyway. I was counting on you. We needed you to carry on. And here you up and go away, without warning us and without turning back. You've gone down a one-way street. You've abandoned us in the middle of our journey. You're not interested in your parents. You think you'll get along better with the dead, but in joining them you turn to ashes yourself. Now you can see that spirits are only ashes. Don't you feel a little regret? Yes, yes, I know you regret it, you must regret it. How dare you do such a thing to me? You hit too hard, you selfish little girl. I was ready to forgive you everything. You could have shaken up the earth and the sky if it pleased you to contradict your parents and defy our traditions. I wouldn't have said a thing, I'd have closed my eyes, that's all. You could have slept with anyone, become a whore if you liked. I wouldn't have stopped you anymore. I would have submitted to my destiny, submitted to you, my daughter, my sovereign daughter. But this time, you've really gone over the line. You can't retrace your steps anymore. Isn't that right, you won't be coming back?"

She heads toward the exit. She opens her hands, brings them to her nose to examine them up close. She finds a light layer of dust on them and begins to rub them attentively.

IT WAS SATURDAY. I WAS WANDERING AROUND MY
favorite street, filled with people already dressed in their
Sunday best. Lovers were walking hand in hand. Single
girls were strolling with their parents, somber looks on
their faces. People glanced curiously at my suitcase, then
at me. In the streets of this city, people ate ice cream,
people shook hands, people laughed, but no one carried
a suitcase. Shoes pounded the pavement in an endless
rhythm. The rays of the setting sun shone on coiffed
heads. How dignified and satisfied these people seemed,
and how well integrated into their surroundings. They
loved their mothers, no doubt, and later on they could
go home.

I opened the door to the Happiness Café. I would have liked to hide my suitcase somewhere, but the proprietress noticed it right away. She could take in everything at a glance, a skill she needed to catch customers who tried to leave without paying.

"What's this?" she asked. "Going on a trip?"

When I nodded, she let out a cry that turned every head.

"Quick! Bring the young lady a tea, she's in a hurry."

She thought departures were always rushed. I headed for my usual place with a falsely accelerated step, admiring eyes upon me. The proprietress, who had never left the city in her life, came to take my order personally.

"I'm going very far away this time," I told her. "And I'm never coming back."

"Don't joke around!" she protested. "How can you do that to me? My customers always come back."

"We may see each other again in the distant future."

She suggested I order some spring rolls to go with the tea.

Night fell. The pedestrians dispersed in a swirl of wind. Someone closed the windows. With the lights on, the street already seemed less real than earlier. The customers came and went. I ordered two spring rolls. They were served still dripping with oil. I wolfed them down. I had a bit of a stomachache. But I was happy not to have to eat at home anymore. I would be free to eat a lot or not at all. I would spare myself the rice tonight! At home, we only went without rice on special occasions: weddings, funerals, or the springtime festival. From now on, I could maintain the illusion that every day was a big occasion. I was especially happy to finally be able to pay for my meals myself. No longer would I have to give my whole salary to Mother, who had decided to deposit it in the bank to build up my dowry instead of making me pay room and board. It was almost humiliating how this dowry had chained me to Mother. It had deprived me of the pleasure of eating meat and made me feel I'd worked for years at a boring job without even managing to feed myself. As if I had worked all this time only to prepare for my marriage. As a result, Chun's advances lost all their romance in my eyes. It seemed to me that the love affairs I'd had in the past were compromised from the start by the preparation of this dowry. But when I thought about it, Mother's actions weren't so strange after all. A dowry prepared before love arrived was as necessary as a coffin assembled before the first signs of death. One's life might end in a thousand ways, but the coffin, as a future or final point in one's journey, was essential. For Mother the dowry was a necessity, the love a condition.

I was satisfied with my reasoning. Maybe it wasn't such a bad idea to prepare a dowry for oneself. Now that I was going to have my whole salary at my disposal, I wouldn't know what to do with it. I wasn't in the habit of spending. "What else can you complain about?" Mother had said. "I always gave you the necessities!" And it was true. I had no idea what might exist beyond necessities. If my suicide effort failed, perhaps I'd start eating meat or fish more often. And love? Wasn't it a little much to want love when you already had a dowry, and probably a room besides? "Look for your love in novels," said Hua, "but not in life, or you'll spoil everything!" Mother seemed to know all about this. Was that why she always focused on necessities and made it her job to protect me, using her will of steel to crush my illusions one by one?

NOW THAT I had left home, I could have forgotten Mother, dropped my plan for vengeance, and gotten on with my life. But from deep in my head, her eyes were upon me. Her voice, shrill and firm, filled my ears as well. For the moment, Uncle Pan's illness was distracting her. But as soon as she found the time and energy, she would turn back to me and pounce. One day, we had a memorable conversation:

"I want to be me, Mother."

"You can't be you without being my daughter."

"I'm me first."

"You lived in my belly first."

"I want to be alone now."

"No one is ever alone. You're always someone's son or daughter. Someone's husband or wife. Someone's mother or father. Someone's neighbor or countryman. You always belong to something. We're social animals. Other people are our oxygen. You can't do without them if you want to survive. Even ants understand that better than you do."

"What if I don't want to survive?"

"Do what you want. But you can't deny that I'm your mother and that your father is your father. That, no. Never. Didn't your grandmother teach you that? Even when we're dead, our spirit continues to belong to the family."

"And Lord Nilou?"

"Only our ghost follows him."

"But, Mother, please, try to think of it as if I had never existed, either in your belly or in the world."

"How can I? As soon as you bring a child into the world, you're condemned for life. You're condemned to watch over the child. Even if our spirit rejects the child, our body commands it. You have to be a mother to understand."

So there was no solution. It was impossible not to belong to something. At least so long as I was alive.

•　　•　　•

THE PROPRIETRESS asked me the time of my departure. I admitted that I didn't know exactly. She looked at me with a pained expression and I realized I had stayed too long. It was ten o'clock and the restaurant was almost empty. I promised her I'd leave soon. I planned to get it over with that evening, because I didn't know where to spend the night. I began to write a farewell letter. I tried to be as hypocritical as possible:

"Dear Mother, I am going to die now. Would it surprise you to know I was dying for you, just as others die for their beloved? I am going to make this extravagant gesture, a stupid gesture, you would say, because I can find no better way of showing you my devotion. I'm not very eloquent, as you know. You're all I think about, Mother, for a reason that has now become clear: I would be nothing at all if you hadn't formed me with your blood and guided me with your powerful vision. My gratitude to you is immense. In the old days, they sacrificed children for the good of the community. Today, if my act can make up for all the stupid things I've done that have made you suffer, my soul will be at peace. I never dared confess my love for you, Mother, in the name of the discretion you hold so dear. Now what more have I to fear? So I shall tell you a thousand times: Mother, I love you."

I folded the sheet of paper carefully and placed it in my bag, between my bottles. I phoned home, my hands trembling. Grandmother picked up. Mother wasn't there. Uncle Pan had had a sudden attack and had been sent to the hospital in an ambulance. Grandmother didn't know which hospital. Father was already asleep.

I had to find Mother. I had to wait. I pressed a hand to my purse with the rattling bottles inside. I swallowed my saliva.

The waiter brought the check. The proprietress had dropped her smile. But the heat of the tables and chairs held me back. I hesitated a few moments longer and left.

I HEADED FOR THE TRAIN STATION, WHERE I COULD play the real traveler. I could also find a place to stay. I quickened my step. The streets were deserted. I was alone with my shadow. Lights shone from windows. I turned up the collar of my coat. A cat crossed the street and plunged into an alley. The train station was a few yards away. Stories of criminal acts suddenly crossed my mind. I began to run, which did me good: I wasn't cold anymore and I appeared more normal. Mother's voice, mixed with the cold air, slapped me in the face.

To survive, my child, you have to constantly adjust the movements of your body and your mind. It's important to know when to run and when to climb, when to bend and when to straighten, when to think and when to sleep. Watch the direction of the wind. Never sail against the current. Lately I've gotten the impression that you're too puffed up around your parents, for instance. Make yourself smaller, lower your eyes, more, more . . . that's right, like that. That posture's not so bad, is it? Not too painful? You'll get used to it. I don't spoil my children. It's for your own good, you know. It's a good exercise that will help you succeed in life, in marriage and your work . . .

I liked the commotion in the train station. People were sprawled on the ground in front of the entrance, so many you had to be careful not to step on them. Most of them were from the provinces and didn't have the money for a hotel room, even if their train wasn't leaving until the next morning or later. I wanted a place among these foreigners. I felt good there. Like them, I wasn't in my hometown. I was only passing through. They smoked strong leaves under my nose and yelled in my ear with confusing accents. I smiled. The young girl near me had teeth the color of the sun. She kept asking me questions. I didn't answer on account of my local accent. I wasn't from around here, but I had the accent. As soon as I opened my mouth, these people would know that I was different and would find it strange that I should be among them, where I wasn't meant to be.

Every so often someone left. The others followed along with envious eyes. That person would hasten toward the train, his heart already elsewhere. Those who remained checked their tickets and their watches once again.

I had no watch and no ticket.

After midnight, the train station grew calmer and colder. Unable to sleep, I felt like rewriting my letter. I wanted to tell Mother, in an uncalculated, unrestrained manner, that I missed my little room, my prison. I was actually separated from her for the first time. I imagined her anger and her concern. We were always together. We ate at the same table, went to the same movies and the same stores. She liked to advise me on which clothes to buy and I couldn't seem to make a decision without her. Had the superabundance of her advice made me indecisive, or had my indecisiveness prompted her to advise me constantly? I couldn't separate the cause from the effect. What was the point anyway? Maybe it was only natural for me to need advice and for Mother to give it. A mother should have the milk her daughter needs. I congratulated myself on discovering this comparison and was sure that Mother would like to hear it, especially now that she would have to get used to going out without me, without a daughter, alone in the crowd.

At the crack of dawn I hurried to leave this train station overrun with travelers. Mother would never turn up here. With her attachments to her husband, her brother, her colleagues, her neighbors, and especially her daughter, Mother had neither the time nor the desire to travel.

Besides, did she really need to travel to see the world? A mother didn't visit the world, she carried it. She had created a child. And she had done it from nothing. She'd had only vegetables, or almost, to fill her stomach, and her belly had swelled up anyway. Something had taken shape there, something that qualified as human. An evolution had taken place inside her body. Her bowels had recorded every pain. As a result, they had become historical organs. Today, the fruit of this evolution stood before her, a cruel irony, green and useless, bitter and impure. She looked at her daughter and she understood the world. The wise man didn't need to cross his threshold to become wise. And so she had unclasped her hands. She preferred to set her child free. She had wasted her time. Now she wanted to give up on the future because —what could she do?—she was living in a time of ingratitude.

I didn't know where else to go, so I returned to the Happiness Café.

MY TEA HAD GONE COLD LONG AGO. I WAS STARING AT the bottom of my cup with its variations of leaves. Outside, the sun was shining oppressively. I reread my letter. A confused and unexpected feeling rose in my throat, which quickly transformed itself into warm tears. Doesn't everything turn to water in the end? The letter too was getting wetter. This deceitful letter, this false declaration of love to Mother now seemed to me something sincere. I had wanted to strike her hard—oh, how she deserved it!—but it hurt me even before it hurt her. I was racked with pain. I bowed under the blows by which I would destroy Mother upon destroying myself.

One must never betray one's mother; Mother had warned me.

Bringing me a fresh pot of tea, the waiter—perhaps on purpose—knocked over an open bottle I had placed on the table. White pills rolled to the ground like shooting stars and were crushed by innocent feet. I would have to wait a little while longer. I still didn't know if this was the right time and the right place. I still had to eat my last spring roll, listen for the last time to the racket the regulars made, and gaze once more through the window at the streaking colors of the street. The proprietress glanced at me surreptitiously. I sent her a smile. "I haven't left yet because I lost my ticket," I shouted. She acted as if she didn't hear me, turned to other customers, and sneered loudly, about what I don't know.

At that moment, a shadow fell through the window next to me. The pills that had survived turned a grayish color. Without lifting my eyes, I knew it was Chun. He had his own way of appearing. Our eyes wouldn't have met that day if he hadn't suddenly turned the corner of a narrow alley on his bicycle, if he hadn't loomed up in front of me, hiding the sun behind his back, making me cry out in alarm, suddenly making me very lost, very womanly, very desirable. And now he was motioning stupidly behind the window. He was so close and so far. I smiled at him. Today I was ready to smile at everyone.

His eyes fixed on my bottles and my tea; his face grew moist. I filled my cup and brought it to my lips cautiously, but was stung by the heat anyway. This destroyed my good mood. I felt a resounding irritation against this tea, against this wounding liquid which refused to make its way down my throat, against this hostile café where I was being spied on, against Chun, who seemed to be born to interfere where I wasn't expecting him. On my table I saw the shadow grow more and more agitated. I had a sense of foreboding. This shadow, following me, swallowing me through the window, reminded me of Mother. She too was both loving and oppressive. I had to postpone my plan once more. I put the bottles back in my purse. I crumpled the letter and tossed it into a nearby wastebasket.

He entered the café and whispered something to the proprietress. She turned pale and picked up the phone. Chun sat down opposite me uninvited. He smiled as if nothing were happening. As if he hadn't noticed the pills, hadn't cried, and hadn't betrayed me by talking to the proprietress about me. As if he wasn't Mother's accomplice. He smiled because he thought he knew my destiny better than I did. I told him I had to go to the bathroom. I noticed a glimmer of suspicion in his eyes. He lifted his arm as if to prevent me from leaving the table. But he resigned himself to it, heaving a sigh that was almost touching.

I STILL hear his sigh rolling through space. I see his shadow, like a cloud, hovering over me. When the wind rises, I lose consciousness and have the impression of being swallowed.

WHEN I PASSED THE PROPRIETRESS, I HEARD HER SAY into the phone that it hadn't happened yet but urgent measures seemed to be required. I guessed she was talking about me. Probably to the police. Or to Mother, whom she knew very well. Or even to the psychiatric hospital. Or to the emergency room where they pumped your stomach. My protests there would be in vain—no one believes a muddled mind. They might even open my stomach to be sure of its purity. Mother wouldn't hesitate to sign the release form for this. She had every right, and they all knew it. She would brag of having given life to me twice. Later, she would try to console me, saying that it was nothing to have your belly opened: she had undergone the same thing. She would be delighted to see me with a scar on my stomach just like hers; that way, I would resemble her all the more.

I dashed outside. Things were turning ugly. I should have been more wary of Chun. He was running after me. I could hear his obstinate steps. He didn't want to let me go. I turned around and found him terrifying; with the swollen veins on his forehead, he reminded me of a ruthless hunter. He was running after me the way Mother did, with determination. I suspected he had been sent by Mother or that the very incarnation of Mother was following me. I tried to shake him. I looked at him tenderly, but he didn't react. To allow himself to be distracted at such a moment would be ridiculous. Besides, he couldn't see my face anymore. I had become a moving shape for him to catch. Prey have no faces; true hunters don't study moods. They measure only speed. They live outside of others and themselves. They exist completely and solely in time. Fear passed through my body and descended into my legs. They became heavy quickly. I stumbled. But I forced myself to go on. I still hoped to get away from him. How I wished I hadn't accepted the blood-red scarf he had wrapped around my neck one Sunday afternoon, the sky filled with autumn dust. I had the impression I was wearing that scarf this very moment. I was hot. The scarf felt tighter and tighter and hurt my throat. Its color blinded me. I tried to hide in the crowd. At that point Chun began shouting, "Stop that girl!"

He pointed his merciless finger in my direction as if I were an enemy. The others got excited. "Why? Did she steal something from you?"

I left the hostile sidewalk. I descended toward the bicycles, the cars, the trucks, and the buses. I couldn't tell in which direction they were going. The important thing was to grab on to something, to protect myself from the madman chasing me. I honestly couldn't lift my feet anymore. So I began to crawl. The surface of the pavement was reassuringly hard. Finally a solid island, the only thing that didn't move. With the pedestrians shouting their heads off on the sidewalk, the drivers turned to look at them, no doubt intrigued and amused. When the truck rolled over me, it resembled a black, upside-down mountain. Or rather, it was I who plunged into this shadow more enormous than Chun's. He was there when I opened my eyes. A liquid, oh!, more liquid, but this time thicker, flowed slowly down his face. I looked at him sadly. I told him, "This isn't what I wanted."

I didn't hear my last words. I don't think the others did either. A final word, a final series of sounds, a final wish was thus lost forever. My head had become chaotic. Red and black were circulating at a preposterous speed. I managed nonetheless to keep my eyes open. The light around me became more and more intense. The street was blindingly white. The sun began devouring my body. Time was running short. I was worried. I looked for Mother, I hoped she would find my letter at least. But all I could see was Chun's face bending over me. It was filled with the pain of a master who's been robbed. Once again, I saw an expression of despair and reproach similar to Mother's.

I REMEMBER THAT CHUN, STANDING ON THE EDGE OF
the sidewalk, screamed, "Idiot!" Or perhaps it was "Idi-
ots!" I don't know if he was talking about the driver
whose vehicle was rolling over my hips, or about me,
whose flesh was on the verge of losing its texture. Or
about himself, who should have let me swallow the pills
first and then had my stomach pumped, rather than deliver me like this to the weight of the wheels that were
destroying my guts. Or about Mother, who had been
careless enough to allow me to buy pills and, especially,
who had given birth to a girl destined to torment him.

I wouldn't be really angry if he called me an idiot. I
have a hard time believing, even now, that my life ended

so stupidly. An accident that blocks traffic. Like my father's. A fluke. A mediocre ending, without will or emo-
tion. Without importance or depth. A lightweight death
that will be remembered neither for better nor for worse.
I now wonder whether I was the one who wanted death
or if death chose me. I'll have to check Lord Nilou's list.
Was it already my turn anyway? Did he send me into
an enemy womb in order to have me back sooner?

By now he should have come to guide me and written
me up. But he still hasn't come. How long have I been
floating here? I have never seen such a neutral place, so
devoid of color, of scent and taste, of shape, weight and
heat. And yet, isn't this what I had wanted? Sterile eternity and a flowerless garden.

Not only did I live badly, I think, I died badly. By
crushing my body, that stupid truck completely transformed the appearance of things. Mother has an easier
time handling an accident than a suicide. Her conscience
won't be disturbed so long as she doesn't believe herself
to be the direct cause of my death. That's why she's able
to stand during these days of mourning. Her back doesn't
curve as much as I had hoped. The front of her shirt is
drenched in tears, but that's not enough to console me.
Tears are soothing anyway. When Mother used to make
me suffer, I had no tears. My eyes were dry and empty.
But my heart bled. I told Mother my heart was bleeding
but she didn't want to hear it. She said I was exagger-

ating. I knew she would never believe me, precisely because I wasn't exaggerating enough. So I thought of pills. Now I understand that our mother is our destiny. You can't turn away from your mother without turning away from yourself. When you lose your mother, you lose your strength and your shelter, you're delivered to the terrifying chill of the unknown and your projects accidentally shatter in a thousand pieces. I wanted to attack Mother, so my bones broke against her bones and my soul became a dog without a master. Fallen leaves return to their roots, dead men gather around Lord Nilou. But traitors to their mothers will continue to be vagabonds, whether dead or alive, to be excluded from the cycle of life, to be everywhere and nowhere. To not be.

WITHOUT LORD NILOU, I DON'T KNOW WHERE TO GO. I no longer recognize left or right, high or low. There are no directions anymore. In the past, I sought a direction. I wanted to make choices. I wanted to choose a mother, or at least to change her to my liking. I wanted to choose a man. I wanted to choose between life and death, as well as the means of my death. Now I have been delivered not only of my body but of all these choices, choices which used to cause me so much sorrow but have now become as insignificant as the powder of my flesh.

• • •

PEOPLE COME and go, emitting a thick smoke that separates me from them. I can hardly see what prompts them to act. Mother continues to eat, move her lips and limbs, and sleep. She says things I barely understand. I have the impression she's talking about me. Already she seems less sad. I doubt she would have suffered more even if I had succeeded in my suicide. None of it matters, though. My hatred burned up in the oven where they tossed my body. Mother has that candor of the living, who believe that death is only an accident. From the ancestors' ruins rise waves of dust bearing generations of waste; they roll around her and whiten her hair without her knowing it. I discover for the first time that Mother is in fact as innocent and vulnerable as the others. She continues to live. She keeps to her schedule. She walks with a heroic step and sits like a mountain. She sleeps a deep sleep. She ignores the dust that is filling her and all that surrounds her. When the dust becomes too thick, the water of the sea will invade the city and the bodies will be cleansed. I see Mother in the belly of a fish. And I see myself in Mother's belly. We ate so many fish. Mother now seems less solid to me. I prefer her this way. I would like to tell her so, but it's too late. I suppose it's for the best.

Chun has finally gone out with a girl. I see them walking side by side on the very street down which he chased me so furiously. Their sleeves brush against each other.

He seems to want to avoid her fleshy arm, since his memory of me is still present. But he, she, and I all know that he will soon take this arm, for how many more seasons no one knows. The sun shines in their eyes and they smile. They strike me as the most beautiful couple I have ever seen.

Some decline rapidly. Father spends more and more time in bed. Grandmother is beginning to lose her hair, her memory, and her teeth. Uncle Pan moves to the hospital, where enormous women await their babies. And Mother has bought a young bird and placed it in a cage hung from the window. She speaks to it sometimes. A new tenderness blossoms on her face, erasing a worn sadness. She licks her wounds, takes care of herself courageously. She continues to love in her way. She begins to train and discipline her bird, to console herself for her previous failure, to create some kind of future for herself, to bequeath her estate and ensure continuity to her life. No one in her place could behave any differently. You have to settle up as best you can. I find what she is doing quite moving.

But maybe that woman next to the birdcage isn't her. I'm not quite sure I recognize her. I'm beginning to lose my sight, to confuse family and strangers, people and animals, beings and things. And I can no longer tell the difference between today and yesterday. I see no tomorrow. I realize then that I am truly dead. When you're alive, you evaluate time. You count the years, the seasons, the days, and the seconds. Nothing escapes this calculation. Even the light and the sand have an age. That way, you give yourself the impression of possessing a considerable number of seasons, even more days and countless seconds. You make sure you have the time to do everything, to love and to hate, to build and to destroy. To participate in all this, you need a living body. That means I'm out. What a relief to be out of this endless game, to be protected from time, from the rhythmic bubbling up of love and bitterness, pleasure and pain, birth and death, parents and children . . . But how can you appreciate this newfound happiness, its timelessness and emptiness, without having lived within time, without having suffocated in its richness? How can you feel the glacial joy of the foreign without having once had a homeland? And how can you learn to get rid of a mother without ever having been born? To be the child of a woman is an opportunity that enables you to experience the happiness of not being one. An opportunity one must be extremely grateful for.

I hurry to contemplate this city, which has become increasingly hazy, distant, and incomprehensible. Familiar things float around me, the streets and the river, mothers and rats, decomposing and changing colors. And I too am floating. I go very far away. For the first and last time, no doubt, I listen to the murmur of the Alps,

I touch the Saharan heat, I drink the bitter waters of the Pacific. It all seems so beautiful when there are no more choices to make, when you love without an object, when Lord Nilou isn't coming, when you have no destiny.

I still hear voices speaking of me, warily or sympathetically, since the box that contains a part of my body's ashes is still in its place in the cemetery, whereas other boxes are already out of place or lost altogether. The light permeates everything, drunk and triumphant. The landscape recedes, shrinks, and fades. I can't see anything. I can't see Mother. I have no one anymore, neither Mother nor Lord Nilou. My memory of Mother melts into the uniform light. My memory evaporates like the cloud that carries me. Through the fog of this memory, like an enchanted lament, comes the last human voice, maybe the cry of an infant:

"Mother!"